REID'S REDEMPTION

SARA CELI

Published by Lowe Interactive Media, LLC
Copyright ©2019 by Sara Celi

First Edition: May 2019
Library of Congress Cataloging-in-Publication Data
Reid's Redemption / Sara Celi – 1st ed
ISBN-13: 978-1099952272

For Ohio.

PROLOGUE

Five Years Ago

Reid Powell

"Y ou're out of your mind, Logan. You've gone crazy," Reid Powell said from the foyer. "What did you take? What have you *been* taking?"

"Nothing." Logan shoved his balled fists into the pockets of dirty jeans. Once, the pair had been a tight fit. Now, he was so skinny they threatened to slide down his hips. "Okay, just the Adderall. I have a prescription for that. You know how I am with my ADHD, and—"

"Bullshit." Reid stepped closer to Logan. "Tell me what you did."

"Nothing. I didn't do *anything*."

"I'm so tired of your lies."

Reid's jaw locked in anger. He had enabled Logan for too long, and that needed to end. Immediately. No more, no matter how much it hurt. One of their father's dying wishes had been that Reid take care of Logan, and that meant stopping his brother's codependency. *Today.*

"I want to know what you took, Logan. *Now.*"

Reid's younger brother shifted back and forth on two wobbly legs. "Some vodka, okay? And I've been smoking."

"Heroin. You've been smoking heroin again, haven't you?"

The word "heroin" tasted unnaturally bitter on Reid's tongue, but each time it escaped his lips, it tasted less foreign than the last. Saying it made it real, and Reid needed the clarity that came from that fact. *Junkie. My brother is a junkie. He's been one for months—almost a year.* That sounded unnatural, too, but they were long past the point of *anything* in their lives being natural. Natural died over a decade earlier, on the day their dad padlocked Powell Steel. Natural died brain cancer took their father, and then a heart attack took their mother, all within the past three tumultuous years. And natural died when Logan began avoiding his problems by using hard drugs.

"Did you mix the heroin with anything else?" Reid asked.

Anything like meth?

Logan shrugged, and Reid knew his answer. *Yes.* "I just want what's mine, okay?"

This. Always money. Always greed. Always a failure to see anything outside his own pain. *When the hell will he grow up?*

"Christ, you're a Powell, for fuck's sake." Reid's frustration with his younger brother grew with every hollow breath. "You don't have to worry about money."

Logan 's gaze shifted toward the open front door, which let in the stale, crisp air that came with the waning days of an Ohio autumn. "You don't understand. You never did." He looked at his brother. "I need some cash. Now."

Need. There it was. Again.

Reid sighed as he felt the heaviness of that moment surround them both. No matter how many books he read, how many articles he scanned, he'd never accept the naked selfishness that came with his brother using drugs. It shamed him to see how much Logan put his cravings above everything else. What a mess their lives had become.

"What about that two fifty I gave you three days ago?"

"That was a start." Sweat beaded on Logan's brow. He was shaky, clammy, and pale. He breathed like a man who'd run three miles at his fastest pace. "But I have a few other—"

"No." Reid didn't know how much longer he'd be able to suppress the ball of frustration in his stomach. "I'm tired of doing this. Tired of bailing you out of whatever trouble you get into."

"I'm just asking—"

"You're not asking. You're *demanding*."

"Come on, man." Logan's eyelids looked heavy, and he spoke slowly. "Don't be an asshole."

"I'm not."

"We're brothers. Family."

"You don't act like we are anymore. All you do is take."

Reid braced his hand on the open-door frame that divided the living room from the foyer. The smooth wood was a throwback to another era, when the Powells entertained the wealthiest people in Allen, Ohio, and threw dinner parties that rivaled any in Cleveland or Pittsburgh. But that had all been eons ago. The parties, champagne, and steak dinners all disappeared when the steel mill shut its doors. Now the brothers only had the aging beaux-arts mansion, an inheritance, some dusty antiques, a strip of ancient farmland on the edge of town, and each other.

Most people would have called it more than enough, but not Logan. He'd tossed away what remained in favor of needles, pills, and whatever chemical escapes he could find. Reid suspected it made the burden of being a Powell easier for his younger brother. If Logan dulled the sharpness of the family failures, he could get through the day. *Survive.*

"I don't need much, Reid. Just a small—"

"No. I'm trying to hold you accountable for your actions," Reid added. "Someone needs to."

"I can take care of myself," Logan replied through gritted teeth.

The brothers stood in the hall, locked in a stalemate for a breath that felt like it lasted a year. Stubbornness was a Powell trait, and both had a strong dose of it flowing through their veins. As the moments passed, Reid wondered what version of "taking care of myself" meant showing up at your brother's door for handouts. All Reid wanted was for Logan to quit the drugs for good, and to admit he'd made a lifetime of mistakes. Once again, his younger brother was letting him down.

I don't care. I won't give in, Logan.

"Fine," Logan said. "If you won't give me any money, I'll find someone who will." He glared at his brother one last time, turned on a booted heel, and moved toward the front door. "I hate you," he grumbled over his shoulder.

"You don't mean that."

Logan didn't answer. Reid watched his brother bound down the porch steps into the cold afternoon wearing no coat, no scarf, and no hat. When he hit the pavement, Reid made a split-second decision.

He grabbed his navy puffer coat and scarf from the hall bench, then his keys from the glass bowl on the console table. "Don't leave," Reid yelled as he pulled the heavy door shut and locked it. "Logan, stop this."

In the driveway, Logan started his sedan, and Reid called out again. "Don't go."

Still yelling, Reid raced down the front steps in time to stop the car from leaving. He beat on the driver-side window until Logan rolled it down. "What do you want?" He had wide eyes and shaky hands.

"You shouldn't drive." Reid grabbed his brother's diminishing bicep. "You're not in the right frame of mind."

"Too bad," Logan replied. "And you can go fuck yourself. I don't give a damn what you think."

Without rolling up the window, Logan punched the accelerator and sped down the driveway. With one eye on his brother's car, Reid sprinted to his own truck, parked a short distance away. His brother may be a screwed-up junkie, but Reid loved him.

He was family, after all. The only family Reid had left.

A half hour later, a twisted lump of metal that had once been a school bus straddled all four lanes of State Route 23. Eleven people were dead—one adult, ten children. The acrid smell of smoke filled Reid's nostrils. Screams punctuated his ears. In the distance came the sound of an approaching ambulance.

Reid wondered if he was dead, too—and if this was hell.

In a lot of ways, it already was.

CHAPTER ONE

Present Day

Tarryn Long

Two days after I moved to Allen, Ohio, I strode into Country Market searching for four things: protein drinks, milk, eggs, and bread. It was early January, frigid, and in a way, I was on a mission. Getting these items was the one task my father had allowed me to do for him since I'd arrived in town. Despite my insistence that Dad needed family around to help him recover from the stroke he'd suffered in December, he was still trying to convince me to return to Ohio State for the spring semester. He hated that his health had taken such a turn, and that I'd decided to interrupt my studies once he'd been released from the hospital. Even that morning, he'd told me to pack up and head back to school.

But I wasn't going to leave him. Dad needed me, so Allen was where I needed to be. Family first.

"Fancy seeing you here," called a friendly voice as I entered the quiet store. I looked up from my list to find Marlena Moss, the longtime owner. She was older, heavier, and more wrinkled than the last time I saw her. But I shouldn't have been that surprised. It had been too long.

"I didn't realize you still owned this place," I exclaimed. I crossed to Marlena and gave her a quick hug.

"Some things don't change," she said after we pulled apart. "I guess the rumors were right about you. Still, I can't really believe you're back in town."

"Why not?"

"Because you were at Ohio State."

"So?" Leaving school to take care of my dad for a semester hadn't been that hard of a decision. A stroke was serious, especially at his age. I spread a hand. "School can wait."

"What about your scholarship?"

"It will all work itself out. Right now, my family is more important."

"Look at you. So loyal." Marlena studied me. "I keep trying to remember the last time you visited here. It's been forever."

"Well, I'm happy to be here now. Allen has a lot of good memories for me."

She snorted. "Sounds so weird to hear someone say that. These days, no one moves *to* Allen." She shrugged, and sadness pulled at her eyes. "They move away."

Marlena was right.

As a kid, Allen had been a bustling place, full of close-knit life and small-town comradery. My parents divorced when I was six, and while I lived with her in Cincinnati during the school year, I spent every summer in Allen, visiting my dad. I liked playing in the rolling hills and dense forests that made up the outskirts of Victor County too. But I hadn't been to Allen, or the surrounding county for over five years.

Not since...

Now, only the local dairy bar, a few churches, one bar, a diner, two banks, a funeral home, and Country Market remained. The rest of downtown consisted of abandoned buildings, crumbling pavement, and vacant lots full of weeds. The surrounding county didn't look much better. How different it all was.

I put a hand on Marlena's shoulder. "Dad's health is important to me, so I'm not leaving anytime soon."

She smiled but didn't show what remained of her teeth. "How is he today?"

"Been better. Some days he's almost fine. Other days, it's like the reality of it all sets in and he gets so frustrated." I took a few more steps into the store, then pivoted back to her. "You know how it is. The stroke was..."

I trailed off because I didn't know what to say. Shocking? Scary? A wake-up call for me about my father's mortality?

All those descriptions would have fit.

The doctors in Cleveland insisted that Dad should consider himself lucky, that it could have all been far worse. Still, while his condition improved a bit every day, one side of his body was a weakened shell he struggled to control. Fifty-four years old and facing a major life change. He couldn't run his beloved half marathons. Or hunt deer on weekends in the blind he owned in the southern part of the state. And he'd taken an extended leave of absence from his job as the Victor County prosecutor. We weren't sure if he'd ever go back to work. *No, not if. When.*

"All of us were sad to hear about it," Marlena mumbled. "Been praying."

I'd heard it before, from other people in town. I knew I'd hear it again. Praying was something the people of Victor County did a lot of those days. Praying, and holding on to something—a remnant of the past.

"Thank you." I held up my list. "Gotta get these real quick then get back to the house. Nora's about to leave for the day."

"Of course." Marlena nodded. "It's been good of Nora to help your dad out with all his rehab. I'll let you get to it."

She moved back to the first of two registers at the front of the store, and I grabbed a wire basket before heading down the center aisles. Country Market might not have been a big business, but Marlena and her husband Kurt did their best to keep it stocked with all the necessities. The low lighting and simple layout gave it a homey feel, and I savored the casual comfort that came with this being a center of life in the community. If Country Market ever closed, it would be an irreparable blow.

I'd just taken the milk out of the dairy case when the door jangled, and another shopper walked into the store. At first, I didn't look up from my task, but then I heard a sharpness in Marlena's voice at the front.

"We're out of peanut butter. Truck with the shipment comes next week."

I turned my head and found a man with chin-length hair and a threadbare coat standing almost in the place where I'd been moments before. He said something to Marlena I couldn't hear, but she gritted out a tense reply.

"Whatever you need, go ahead and get it. And then get going."

He mumbled an answer, then moved down the first aisle, where he picked up a loaf of bread and a jar of jelly. I stared at him as he moved toward the checkout. There was something about his olive-green jacket, the thick stubble that covered his jaw, and the shaggy brown hair he wore underneath an old orange trucker hat, which obscured his face. He wasn't dirty, but he wasn't clean either. And Marlena's voice had been a warning.

She doesn't like him.

I watched them go through the motions of payment then speak a few more strained words to each other. She kept her attention on him as he left, and her gaze followed him as he walked outside to a dark Ford F-150 truck parked alongside my own Toyota Camry. Once he drove out of the parking lot, she made a clucking sound with her tongue.

"Who was that?" I asked when I arrived at the checkout.

Marlena sneered. "No one."

I put the bread on the counter. "He was someone."

"No one worth a damn." She looked at me. "Trash."

The word echoed in my head; she had said it like a curse. *Trash.* I'd always known Marlena Moss as a friendly woman, a person who had a cheery smile for everyone, no matter what. I may not have grown up in Allen, but I'd always thought of Marlena as the town grandmother. She'd never been the type to look down on anyone.

But there she stood, looking down on this man. Whoever he was, he must have deserved it.

"I'm sorry I asked," I said. "You seemed so upset he was here."

"You might not have realized this, but Allen really changed in your absence," she replied, and for the first time, I saw a steely hardness behind her eyes. "We've been through a lot."

"I know." I gulped. "The accident—"

"No one here likes to talk about that. Too many bad memories." She held up a hand. "Besides, it's not just that. People here… well, let me just say this. Some people don't belong."

"Some people like him?"

"You've been away a long time, Tarryn. You wouldn't understand." She cleared her throat and reached for the egg carton still in my basket. "We just got these in. Very fresh. Your dad will like them."

I knew better than to press her anymore. Instead, I finished the sale and left the store. But the whole drive home, I thought about the man.

Why did people hate him so much?

CHAPTER TWO

Tarryn

Breath pushed in and out of my lungs in a steady rhythm as I ran. *In. Out. In. Out. In.* The crisp air sliced my throat, a reminder that winter had come to rule the Appalachian Mountains and Victor County. The cold weaved around Allen and its outskirts. Snow covered everything in a white blanket.

Still, I kept going.

Despite the move, I hadn't wanted to give up my routine—a morning run of at least three miles, five days a week. I started doing it in high school, when I ran cross country, and kept it going at Ohio State. Exercise helped me focus, and I needed that, especially with the significant changes my life had taken.

I moved through Allen's broken streets, on cracked sidewalk and then to open asphalt. It was just after six in the morning, and the town hadn't yet woken up. I was alone, and I liked it that way. My thoughts, and the music playing on my iPhone, helped me add the miles.

In. Out. In. Out. In…

I was between mile two and three on the edge of town, just off State Route 23, when I saw the sign. The road had given way to rural land, and all I saw was the occasional dirt road and mile markers. Allen was behind me, and nothing lay ahead.

Until I got to the fence.

It lined the road and followed me as I moved. Chain link. Rusty. The occasional hole. It bordered what looked like overgrown, unfarmed property full of scrub bushes and strangled trees. A rolled line of barbed wire extended across the top of the metal. Nothing to really see until I reached a road that peeled off the main road. Springhill Lane, read the small green marker at the edge.

I'd never noticed this street before. Curious, I turned and followed the dirt trail.

Springhill meandered for about a mile through twisted oaks and knotty ash trees. The path, which had only one line of tire tracks, headed away from State Route 23. If anyone came by here, it didn't happen often.

Undeterred, I trudged onward.

The lane ended abruptly with a "No Trespassing" sign, along with a much higher fence. I stopped, then realized a driveway broke off from the lane. And the gravel wound around some scrub before ending at a large white farmhouse and a few outbuildings. The owner liked privacy, no doubt. They lived a significant distance away from the rest of the town, in a county that was ninety percent rural. Interesting.

I don't remember anyone living out here when I was a kid. It's so far from town...

I took a few more steps, intrigued about the house and its occupants. Whoever lived in the farmhouse maintained the outside and took care of the grounds. Unlike the rest of Allen, this property almost sparkled. The chimney pumped with smoke from an inside fireplace. The exterior paint looked fresh, and the bushes around the porch had been trimmed. A few lights illuminated the rooms on the bottom floor of the house.

When I got about a third of the way down the driveway, I stopped.

Alongside the garage, just off to the side of the house, was the dark Ford F-150 I'd seen two days before outside Country Market.

"No way," I muttered to myself.

Perhaps I'd been mistaken. F-150s were common, and plenty of people had trucks in Victor County. It would be easy to confuse one for another. I walked a bit closer, recalling the truck outside the grocery store, comparing it to this one.

Yes, I *was* right.

The distinctive dent on the bumper gave it away. It *was* the F-150 I'd seen. The car driven by the man in the olive-green jacket. The man who'd turned Marlena Moss from friendly to ice cold.

Anxiety and fear pooled in my stomach. I was trespassing, after all, and there was a very clear sign at the end of the lane warning me not to do so. I needed to turn, leave, and head back to the house. Dad needed breakfast, and Nora would be showing up soon. Our day would begin, and we had plenty to do to help my father get better.

But despite the valid arguments, I didn't move. I stared at the house, watching. Wondering.

I don't know how long I remained there. Five minutes. Maybe ten. Numerous times, I considered knocking on the door. Someone had to be inside, and they might be kind—even offer me a cup of coffee or a glass of water. We might have a nice conversation. Strike up a friendship. Be *neighborly*.

In the end, I turned and ran back to the lane, then out to the state highway. Marlena Moss was probably right. Whoever owned that truck wasn't someone worth knowing. *Trash*, she'd said, and the word had been a slur. Maybe it was better to leave well enough alone.

"Oh, hey there," Nora Stephens said as I pushed through the back door and into the kitchen. She held a chocolate protein drink in her hands, and she shook the can a few times. "How was the run?"

"Good." I walked to the refrigerator and retrieved a bottled water from inside. "It's getting colder."

"They say a storm is on the way." Nora nodded at the TV, which had a newscast from Youngstown, a good thirty miles and a lifetime away from Allen. A blonde anchor on the show was baking cookies as part of a featured segment. "Of course, the meteorologists are predicting it for next week, and they always screw up."

"Never try to guess the weather up here." I slid into one of the four chairs that encircled our small breakfast table. "Even I know that one." I gulped some water. "How's Dad this morning?"

"He's okay." She sat across from me and placed the nutrition drink on the nearby plastic placemat. "He still doesn't like these."

"He doesn't have a choice. He has to drink them."

"I know. I keep telling him that." She sighed. "Your dad always was hardheaded. That's what made---*makes* him such a good prosecutor."

"And always questioning what he should have done differently to win the cases he lost."

"Hasn't lost many."

We fell silent for a long moment. She didn't have to say more. The stroke had interrupted so much of my dad's life. It had left him temporarily paralyzed on the left side of his face, and unable to communicate with the booming voice that had once swayed juries during passionate closing arguments. I hoped to God it would one day return, and that I'd see him in the courtroom once again.

But I couldn't be sure.

"I'm glad you came," Nora finally said. "That you moved here to help him." She nodded in the direction of the living room of the house, which had been converted into Dad's rehab room. "I know it's only temporary, but I'm happy about it. He is too. More than he shows."

"Thanks. He told me last night to go back to school again, but it's already too late. I received the official withdrawal notice in my email."

"You *are* going to finish, aren't you?"

"When the time is right, I will. But that's not now."

"He won't forgive you if you don't."

"And I won't forgive myself if I don't stay here." I studied her. Nora was the same age as I was, but her ashen complexion and the dark rings below her eyes made her look years older. She was a world away from the girl I knew as a kid, the one who came over with her family for Fourth of July barbecues. But we'd lost touch in the last few years, and I regretted that. "I was wondering something. Why did you stay in Allen to be a home healthcare nurse?"

"What makes you ask that?"

"You've never had a client ask about it before?"

She shrugged a shoulder. "No, I haven't."

"You could have moved away to do it. Gone to Pittsburgh. Or Cleveland. Or just *away*."

"Like you?" she scoffed, and the right side of her mouth turned upward in a wry smile that some might have mistaken for a grimace. "I see where this is going. You're asking because you think no one would want to stay in northeastern Ohio if they didn't have to. If they had some better option, they'd do that instead, right?"

"No, I—"

"Whatever." She wrinkled her nose. "We know what people think of us. What they *think* they know about the way that we live. That we're just a bunch of factory-worn hillbillies who keep pining away for the good old days, when we had a town full of jobs."

My eyes widened. *Holy shit.* "I didn't mean my question that way, Nora. I'm sorry. Please—"

"It's okay." Her shoulders slumped as if she realized how defensive she'd been. "No, I... I know you didn't mean to upset me." Her voice was heavy, and she crossed her arms. For the first time, I noticed the small tears along the sleeve hems of her purple uniform, and how faded the color seemed. "I just—we're all tired of people making us a pity project. *I'm* tired of it. We don't need that."

She said the word "pity" as if it tasted sourer than a large piece of grapefruit. I didn't know how to reply. I'd struck a pain point without even trying. *Good work, Tarryn.*

"There was a reporter in town last month. Right around the five-year anniversary of the---well, the *incident*. He was from the *Washington Post*. Wanted to... well, they said they wanted to write a book on what happened... anyway, he asked me for an interview, but I refused. I knew it would end up doing no good. Just another write-up about how we were once a thriving area, and now we are one of the most left behind in the country."

I bit my bottom lip. "I'm sorry."

"Me too." Her index finger drew idle circles on the placemat. "I always wanted to help people. And you're right, I could have left, but I stayed in Allen because it's home."

I nodded. "Probably reason enough. Remember those cookouts Dad used to throw in the backyard for the fourth? And during the holidays, your mom made the best pierogies."

"She still does. You know"—a humorless chuckle escaped her lips— "there's plenty of work here for a person like me. The younger folks might be moving away, but the older ones can't."

"And they need you."

"It's kind of nice, when you think about it." Nora stood and snatched the can from the table. "Oh gosh, it's almost time for your dad's physical therapy."

"Want me to help?" I also got up from the breakfast table.

"Not right now." Nora shook her head. "I can handle it."

"I know you can," I replied as I followed her into the living room. "But I came here for *this* reason."

The living room in Dad's house had become a virtual physical therapy fortress. A walker, exercise balls, a massage chair, and a freestanding tray of prescriptions had taken up permanent residence in the room alongside the overstuffed plaid couch and well-loved La-Z-Boy. Dad was watching a round of golf. I winced when I saw it. Golfing was one more thing he might never do again.

"How are you feeling today?" I asked in a cheerful voice.

"Oh... oh... kay," he mumbled. "You... been... running?"

I nodded. "I ended up getting about five miles in."

He answered with a half-smile. "Good."

"I think so too," Nora said as she walked over to the spare laundry basket, which now held an assortment of rehab equipment instead of clean clothes.

I looked at both. "I came here to help you, Dad, and that's what I want to do. Help."

"Don't need." He pointed a shaky finger at his nurse. "Nora... covered."

"Still—"

"Your time... wasted."

It wasn't wasted, but at the moment, I *was* feeling useless. That needed to change.

"Okay. Enough, Dad." I raised my hands. "Nora is going to teach me some of the rehab strengthening exercises to do with you, so you'll have to put up with me here." He rolled his eyes—as best he could—but I didn't miss the small smile he tried to hide. But he did have a point. I did need to do more with my days—I'd always been someone on the go, with more than one thing happening at a time. "I'm staying until you're better, and that's final. And if you don't want my daily help, do you have another suggestion for my days?"

He shrugged his good shoulder. "Maybe... a... job?"

"A job?" Nora snorted as she brought the handgrip and lung exerciser over to my Dad. "In Allen? Good luck. You're going to need it."

"Do... for... me," Dad said.

"Okay," I replied, despite my reservations. Sometimes it was better to just give in to his demands, instead of trying to win an ongoing argument. "I will."

I had come here for the sake of my father. Even though he and Mom divorced, and I didn't spend as much time with him over the years, I'd never felt unwelcome. Allen had literally been my second home. I was one of the fortunate ones where both parents had loved me without fail. *How could I not have come for him?* It's simply what you did for family you love. *Sacrifice.*

During the daytime, he didn't often venture off the property.

He found things were simpler that way. Less painful. The land provided the protection he needed, a simple barrier between himself and everyone else. For a while, having that assurance had made it easier to live. Easier to breathe. Easier to *be*.

He wondered sometimes if anyone noticed how much he'd done to disappear. If they realized how little he impacted their lives now. If they appreciated it.

No, probably not.

He was a scar from a better time, the physical embodiment of what had once been and likely never would be again. He knew that about himself. Seeing him only made things worse for them. He loathed the pain in their eyes, the way they choked out replies and shifted their weight with unease. And sometimes, they acted out in other ways.

Like a few nights before at the grocery store. He shouldn't have gone in there, asking for food he could have ordered online from some big-box store website. He knew better. No matter how much Reid convinced himself that patronizing the business had been a good thing to do, and spending cash there went into the pockets of people who needed it more than he did, his money was still considered dirty money. His family had tainted every single dollar. They had stolen something. The stain would never wash off, no matter how much he scrubbed.

So, the less people remembered him, and the less he interacted with them, the better.

Reid Powell got up from the living room sofa in his farmhouse and headed into the kitchen. As he poured himself a steaming cup of coffee, he surveyed the back twenty acres of the property he owned. From about a hundred yards away, past the lawn and back patio, bare trees and wild scrub stared back at him. Winter was in full swing, and the air felt brisk. A settled grayness already permeated the region. Comforting, in a way.

Still holding his coffee cup, he moved from the kitchen to the front hall. The property gave him plenty to do each day, and he liked that. Reid found freedom in the menial tasks required to keep the place from going to pot—chopping firewood, weeding flower beds, raking leaves, power-washing siding. Today, he wanted to tackle the pine branches he'd hauled into the side yard. Once he sliced all of them into logs, he'd have enough to keep a fire going all winter.

Reid placed his mug on the narrow hall table, then found his work boots and barn jacket in the hall closet. But when he closed the closet door, a chill ran through him. He felt... watched.

Yes, that's exactly what it is.

From his place by the closet, he had a straight view of a woman through the windows that rimmed the front door. *A woman. Here. What the hell?* She was far enough away he figured she didn't see him, but even so, the sheer shock of someone else on the property was enough to raise the small hairs on the back of his neck. Only Walter visited, and even then, it was twice a week. Walter did that purely out of loyalty. And guilt. And for the money that Reid paid.

So, who is this?

Reid sucked in a deep breath and stared at the figure. She wore a pair of running shoes, black leggings, gray sweatshirt, white gloves, and red knit cap. She looked skinny, but not unhealthy, and he barely made out what looked like patrician features, including a sharp nose and square jaw.

For the longest time, he waited for her to draw closer. Maybe she wanted something. Maybe she'd climb the steps and bang on the door. Maybe she'd explain why *she'd* wandered up the lane, when the large signs he'd posted a few years ago deterred almost everyone else.

He stepped toward the front door. What if he opened it?

But then she turned and ran back down the driveway, away from the house. As she grew smaller, he watched her ponytail sway with each bouncing step.

Soon, like everyone else, she was gone. The stillness and irrevocable quiet of Reid's life returned. *As it should.*

CHAPTER THREE

Tarryn

Nora was right. I did need luck.

A month earlier, I had been on track to get my marketing degree. I'd been ready to finish classes and then study like crazy for my end-of-semester exams. I wasn't sure exactly where I'd work when I finished, but I had a 4.0 GPA and was a hard worker, so I knew I'd find something. And then I'd received the phone call from Mom that had changed my immediate trajectory. *Dad had a stroke. Honey, I'm so sorry. He's in the hospital...*

I had money saved up from part-time jobs I'd held both during the summer breaks and at college, so financially I was okay. But I'd be in Allen for the next four months at least, and while I could take some of my courses online if I wanted, the complete break would be a hard pill to swallow. All this had been so unexpected.

In that way, Dad was right. I had to do something, or I'd go crazy. So, I needed a job. Still, I truly didn't care what I did, so long as I wasn't sitting at home annoying my father, and myself.

But no, the job search didn't go well.

Allen didn't have many openings to begin with, and none for someone a semester away from a marketing degree from Ohio State. Hourly employment was about as good as it got, and that was an ugly reminder, too, of how far away the town was from the days of labor unions and plentiful jobs at the steel mill.

Maybe I've been too optimistic about all of this. Maybe I really should have stayed at school. Maybe...

Frustrated, I parked the car in front of Country Market just after four o'clock in the afternoon. I didn't really know if it would work, but Marlena had probably been the kindest person to me since my return, and I thought she might pity me enough to offer me employment.

"It doesn't take that much to run this place," she told me a few moments after I walked into the store. I was nervous when I walked in, but it was as if Marlena had known what I'd come to ask. Empty-handed, no shopping list... She'd seen it before. I was job hunting. At least she hadn't taken one look and simply said, "No." We stood together near the register closest to the automatic front doors.

"This place has been open for thirty years," she added. "A lot of it's on autopilot. Just a few stock boys, myself, and the hubby."

"I figured, but I thought I'd ask anyway."

The swell of defeat rose in my chest. Dad's words in the living room echoed in my head, but so did Nora's. Maybe I should have listened to *her*, not him.

"I'll do whatever you need," I tried. "Anything."

I was used to working and had held a job since I was fifteen. First at the local library as a page, then the mall at a clothing boutique, and finally during the summers between college semesters at a riverboat cruise company based in downtown Cincinnati.

"No job is beneath me."

"I know that. I know what kind of good stock you come from." She cocked her head and narrowed her eyes. "Actually, I'm glad you showed up today."

"You are?"

"The fact is, unfortunately we lost Tom recently, and that means we *do* have a job opening." Her face fell, and her eyes turned sad. "He was our main cashier during the week. Known him since he was a kid, but I had to let him go. At first, I hoped to hold the position for him, but when I'm honest with myself about it, I know I can't."

"Why not?"

"I shouldn't say; I know I'm not supposed to." Marlena glanced around as if to make sure that we were alone, then lowered her voice. "Keep this between us, okay? He has some issues with pain kill—heroin."

"He does?"

Her mouth fell into a hard line. "Let me just put it this way, like a lot of the kids who grow up here, he's troubled. Not a lot of options, and most people can't afford college without loans. So, you go to the military, or you—"

"Take drugs," I finished.

"Yep." She gulped. "Lots of people self-medicating around here. I started carrying Narcan in my purse last year, and I've used it twice. The last time, about two weeks ago."

Marlena didn't have to say more. It was already bad enough. And confirmation of all that I'd heard from my mom about Allen before I decided to leave school. She'd had no problem reminding me just how much the opioid crisis had taken hold in the region, and it was one of her main arguments against moving in with Dad.

"I'm sorry," I managed.

"We all are. Good help is hard to find, and I hope Tom gets better. But I couldn't trust him anymore. You understand that."

"I do, and I'll take the job. Whatever Tom made, that's fine with me."

"You sure?" She raised her eyebrow. "It's only twenty hours a week, or around that. Not much more."

"That's perfect."

"And it's nine bucks an hour. I don't see—"

"I'll take nine dollars. It's not about the money."

But as soon as those words slipped out of my mouth, I regretted saying them. It sounded elitist, snobby even. Who had the pleasure of doing a job just to pass the time, and not *because* of money? Almost no one in Victor County, and I knew that.

"It just that... well, anything I can do to help. Nora's taking such good care of Dad right now, and I feel useless," I explained further. "So, I don't mind pitching in around here. I want to. He wants me to also. Says it's not good for me to hang around the house all day."

"Sounds like the Peter Long I know." She smiled, and the skin around her eyes folded into flabby rows. "And you're on, Tarryn. You can start tomorrow around ten."

With more spring in my step than when I walked in, I pushed out of Country Market a few moments later. I felt good. It was devastating that she'd lost a good employee to drugs, so in a sense, I was helping Marlena out too. That was the thing about small towns. In a bigger city, my new job simply meant I now had employment. In a small town, I was helping a business stay afloat. And it really would help me pass the time in Allen. I had a lot to learn about Dad's care, but I welcomed that challenge, welcomed having a tighter schedule.

Buoyed, I spotted The One-Way Tavern across the street, a longtime watering hole on the town square. I glanced at my watch. Almost four thirty. I had nowhere to be until around six, when Nora left.

I'll stop in. One beer, or a glass of wine to celebrate following Dad's orders. Can't hurt.

The One-Way Tavern occupied the lower floor of a building that had once been Greenup Savings and Trust, Allen's main bank. The copper nameplate of the bank still adorned the space above the entrance in a straight-line art deco font, and the interior of the bar had small details that threw the place back to its money-managing heyday. But while the old copper, low lighting, and bright ads for Budweiser, Heineken, Sam Adams, and Rhinegeist mixed well together, the establishment still couldn't escape its dive-bar feel. Empty peanut shells littered the floor, and I stepped in something sticky as I crossed the threshold.

"Killian's Red," I told the bartender as I sat on one of the weather-beaten stools in front of the long bar on the right side. "Sounds like just what I need."

"Good choice," the man said, and turned away to type my order into a touchscreen to the left of a line of liquors and mixers. His nametag read Ben, but I didn't recognize him.

I did, however, recognize the other man behind the bar. As our eyes met in the fuzzy dimness, a smile spread across his face.

"Tarryn Long," Carter Monroe called out as he strode toward me. "Glad to see you in here. I heard you were in town."

"Got in a few days ago."

"Word travels fast around here. Especially considering who you are."

I broke his gaze and glanced away. "I'm not anyone, Carter. Just a daughter trying to help her dad."

"How is he?"

"Decent today." I looked at him again. "Good days and bad days. I guess that's how it is in the first few months after a stroke."

"I heard the prognosis is good."

"As good as can be expected."

"Well, we were all still very sad to hear about what happened." Carter braced his arms on either side of the bar. He was still handsome, but in a worn, tired way. His hair wasn't as thick, and a few lines crossed his forehead. But he also had enormous, muscular biceps, a flat stomach, and shades of boyishness that reminded me of the kid I once knew from the community pool. "He's a good man, and it will be a shame if he can't keep working. How long will you be in town?"

"Until he gets better. Not too sure, but probably the rest of this semester. The doctors in Cleveland said these things can go either way. He might make a full recovery and get to where he is pretty independent, and he might not, you never know."

"Good you're here, then."

"It *is* good to be here. And Nora is amazing." My beer arrived, and I took a brief swig of the bottle. The bartender mumbled about appetizers on special that evening, then left when I didn't indicate I wanted to order one. "I don't know what we'd do without her help."

"Yes, she's a decent nurse. Nora's done well with that." His gaze roamed my face. "It's really nice to see you again, Tarryn. I never thought we would, after... after all that... plus the scholarship to Ohio State."

"Dad was pretty clear. It was my junior year, and he... he wanted me to stay with Mom in Cincinnati during the summer, instead of coming to stay with him. He said it would be easier on me."

A rueful chuckle escaped Carter's lips. "He always was smart."

"I never got it, though. Looking back, it still doesn't make sense to me." I glanced around the half-empty bar. "He loved Allen enough to stay, but—"

"There's not much worth talking about here anymore." Carter dropped his hands and moved away from my place. "But some people are stubborn. *I* stayed because of my sister."

I cocked my head, remembering her. She was about two years younger than Carter. "How is Laura?"

Carter rubbed a hand across his forehead. "Not good. Lives over in Redbird Estates. Two kids now, and her boyfriend left her a couple of months ago. She works here when she can."

"I didn't realize."

His mouth turned downward. "I don't like the crowd she hangs with. She's... well... she's an adult and she's going to make whatever decisions she wants. But that doesn't mean she's capable of making good ones."

"I'm sorry," I murmured; I didn't really know what to say.

The truth was, Redbird Estates hardly lived up to its name. Instead, it was a small trailer park on the outskirts of Allen, just next to the site of what used to be Powell Steel. Even during my childhood, the units were shabby, with rusted metal skirting, broken steps, and windows papered in aluminum foil to keep the heat inside during the winter, and prying eyes out. Rumors about drugs and domestic violence ran rampant. During my visits, Dad used to forbid me from playing there. "You don't want to know what goes on in Redbird," I remembered him saying. "It's not a good place for a kid."

"When did Laura move there?" I asked.

"About two years ago." Carter shook his head. "And I think about my niece and nephew a lot. What are they growing up in?" He tapped his knuckles on the bar. "Allen is dying off, and that's all there is to say about it. In a few years or so, this place will be extinct."

"Do you really think that?"

"How is the town supposed to survive if no one wants to live here?"

I didn't have a great reply. He was right. The people who remained were remaining for someone. *But how many more generations would there be?*

CHAPTER FOUR

Reid

Sometimes, when he wanted to get away from the property, he drove around Allen and the surrounding township at night. He'd steel himself against the cold, shove himself into the driver's seat, turn on old Jimmy Buffett ballads, and patrol the streets his family used to walk as kings. In some ways, it counted as therapy. In other ways, as torture.

Many nights, he parked on the edge of town square, turned off the engine, and waited. For what, he wasn't sure. For people to come, maybe. Or for life to show itself. Or for the past to stop haunting him like a ghost.

Anything, really.

That evening, he chose the place at the end of a bank of parking spots in front of Country Market. The store would close in less than fifteen minutes, and from his driver's seat, he had a clear view inside. Bright lights highlighted the shabby shelves, and a few people walked in and out, buying groceries, cigarettes, and alcohol. Marlena manned the center register, and a woman he didn't quite recognize worked the one next to her. Together, they waited on the handful of customers.

Reid opened the can of soda located in the console cupholder and downed a long drink. It didn't do much to quench his thirst as he watched the mundane banality of life pass in a silent play before him. He was a voyeur, and he knew it, but the connections between everyone else and himself had been irreparably broken, and he didn't have the foggiest idea how to repair them. Better to stay away from others, and away from the horrid past. Getting too close to them meant getting too close to the things he'd rather not address.

Reid sipped more soda and watched the end-of-the-evening tableau in the grocery store. Five minutes passed, then ten. And around that time, he heard a commotion. A scuffle maybe, or a fight. Either way, it was happening in the alley between the grocery store and the empty building that had once housed the county's most prestigious law firm. He turned his head and focused on the noise. It grew louder and more frantic with each passing millisecond.

Probably better to not get involved. Keep to yourself.

No need to jump out of the truck and be a hero. The people of Allen didn't want those anyway. They wanted villains to blame for their pain and devils to crucify.

And yet, as he sat there, the screaming pierced his ears. The agony behind the noise wrapped around his lungs. Anxiety in his heart grew. Whoever made those sounds was in trouble. He couldn't let that go by. He couldn't turn away, could he?

No, I can't. I won't.

With barely another thought, Reid yanked the hood over his head, tied the strings tight around his chin, and jumped out of his truck, locking it as he went. In a few steps, he found them.

"What can I tell you?" a woman screeched at the other end of the alley. "I don't have the money."

"Well, you owe me," the man replied, and shoved her so hard against the brick wall she yelped.

"It was just one hit."

"Like I told you, bitch. I don't do consignment." She groaned and the scuffle grew louder. "You gotta pay up."

"Give me more time," she replied. "I can make it up to you."

A chill ran though Reid as he got close enough to see the woman's face for the first time. *Laura. Laura Monroe.*

"Stop," Reid shouted, surprising even himself as the word leapt out of his mouth. "Stop *right* now." Hands shoved into his hoodie, he jogged toward the couple. He snarled at the man. "Let her go."

"Who the hell are you?" Still holding Laura, the man spit on the cracked pavement. "This isn't any of your business, asshole."

"Sure is."

Reid lunged forward and made three swift movements. Within seconds, he'd moved the guy away from Laura, pinning him to the crumbling wall.

"Don't ever treat a person like that again." Reid squeezed the man's neck just tight enough to push the air out of his lungs, but not enough to make him pass out.

"Everyone in Allen could hear her scream. Get the fuck out of here."

The man coughed out an inaudible reply.

"What? You got something to say?"

"Bu—but—"

The stranger tried to wiggle free, but Reid was strong. Years of hard work strong.

"I said, get the fuck out of here."

"You… you…"

"You're a sniveling jerkoff. Do yourself a favor and get the hell out of here." Reid tightened his grip, but only applied enough pressure to make the man struggle some more. He hadn't come here to kill him, though he knew he could. "And don't ever do this again to anybody. *Ever.* Got that?"

The man nodded and gulped some air.

"Good." Reid eased his grip. "Now, go."

The man struggled away, then grasped his strangled neck. He looked at both Reid and the woman as he scrambled farther from them. "Don't know who the hell you are, man, but you're one sick fuck."

"What did I say?" Reid replied.

The man grumbled, turned, and ran down the alley, away from Reid and Laura.

Once they were alone, Reid turned his attention to Laura. He'd never spent much time with the Monroe family, but he'd once been school friends with her brother, Carter. *Once.* The woman in front of him did *not* resemble her former self. *She looks so… beaten. So… lost.*

"Are you okay?" he asked in his deepest voice, thankful for the darkness, the chilly night air, and the way shadows danced in the alley. He didn't want her to recognize him. That might cause more problems.

Laura leaned against the wall opposite from him, breathing hard. She was too thin, and she shivered. A streak of pink hair dye broke up her otherwise dirty hair. Reid wondered when she'd last had a good meal.

"I think I'll be fine," she said between jagged breaths. She braced her hands on her knees and didn't meet his eyes. "But he might come back."

"I know that," Reid replied. "And I don't plan on being here if he does." He sighed. "Whatever that was... I'm not sure I want to know why he attacked you."

Laura looked up finally, and the dim light that made its way through the alley showed him what he feared. Too ravenous. Too haunted. Her eyelids were too heavy and her arms too bony.

That altercation had been the back end of a drug deal.

"What kind of stuff was it?" Reid asked. "Heroin?"

She shook her head.

"Fentanyl?"

Laura nodded.

A low curse escaped Reid's lips. *Fuck.* Living in Allen over the last few years should have made him expect that answer, but it still stung when someone admitted they'd given their life over to a substance that would only end up killing them. Heroin was bad, but fentanyl was worse. Fentanyl had one hundred times the potency of regular, street-ready heroin.

Goddamn it.

He'd been down this road before. He didn't want to walk it again.

"Do you need anything?" he asked, thinking of the Narcan kit he carried in the glove box of his truck. This didn't look like an overdose, but he couldn't be sure. Some addicts built up enough tolerance that they managed regular tasks, like some sick version of the walking dead.

"I'm fine," Laura mumbled. "Fine."

"Good."

He gave Laura one more long look. She was far from okay, but she was alive. She'd wake up tomorrow, and perhaps only have a few bruises instead of major scars. It was the best he could do for her.

"Try to take care of yourself," he said before he left her alone in the alley.

When Reid got back in the car, he was still breathing hard, his heart pounding, threatening to jump out of his chest. He turned on the truck and willed himself to calm down. It wasn't easy.

And then a movement near the grocery store caught his eye.

The blonde behind the register a few moments before walked out of the automatic front doors. From his parking space, Reid had a clear view of her—long hair in a ponytail, ball cap, black leggings, and large puffer coat. It was her—the woman he'd seen on his property about a week earlier.

She headed to a Toyota Camry parked three spaces from him. When she pulled the car out of the lot, he decided to follow her.

Reid knew what he was doing was creepy. Almost stalker level. Not normal to say the least. But for too long, he'd lived away from the people of Allen, even as the moments of his life passed in tandem with theirs. It was almost as if he'd *forgotten* how to be human. And he felt compelled to follow her.

This woman—she was new. Different. Gleaming, in some way, as if she still had a coating of fresh optimism that hadn't been dulled by years of factory closings, cold upper-Midwest winters, national derision, and drug use. She *shined.*

Plus, he knew she was a fan of trespassing. *A rule breaker, maybe, but not the harmful rules.* Reid was a rule breaker too.

They drove through town, winding their way around a few streets until they reached West Oak Street, one of the nicer, better kept parts of Allen. He kept his truck fifty feet or so behind her, careful not to give any indication that his travel on the street was anything but a coincidence.

When she turned into the driveway of a large brick Victorian in the middle of the street, he knew something else about her.

She was Peter Long's daughter. Back in Allen after years away. He also knew her name. Tarryn. Tarryn Long. And he'd been right. She was pure. Someone who would always stand out in Allen.

Holy shit.

CHAPTER FIVE

Tarryn

"**L**et me help you," I said as Herbert Scofield, the main stocker at Country Market, struggled through the swinging doors between the dry goods room of the store and the main sales floor. Herbert carried an oversized case of strawberries, and anyone could see he'd overstepped his abilities. I reached for the wooden crate handle. "There we go."

"Thanks, Miss Tarryn."

He maneuvered a few steps and took the other side. Together, we walked the produce through the aisles and found the fresh fruit section. We set the container on the floor in front of the berries section and unloaded several dozen plastic packages of red, ripe fruit.

"We don't like to do much outsourcing, but sometimes in the winter, you have to," Herbert remarked. "I think these suckers came all the way from Mexico."

"Figures."

He looked at me from underneath tired, hooded eyes. I estimated Herbert was in his sixties, but the bags and folds across his face added a decade or so to his age. "I guess we have to blame globalization for that, right. And maybe, the farm lobby." He picked up one of the packages. "Fake stuff. Engineered food."

I laughed once. "You're probably correct."

He placed the strawberries back in the display case. "I'm wondering, how do you like working here?"

"Oh, it's fine," I said because I couldn't really think of anything else to say. And it *was* that—fine. Working at Country Market over the last two weeks hadn't proven very hard. Just a lot of stocking, straightening, and ringing up various sales. I could have done the job with my eyes closed, but I also still felt grateful I had something to do besides watching daytime television with my dad.

"I'm glad to help here."

"You know what? We needed you." Herbert wiped his hands across the front of his navy apron. The Country Market logo adorned the chest. "In fact, you're probably the best clerk we have."

"I've only been here a couple weeks."

"Hard to find good help these days, and Marlena has complained about that a lot. Not too many people around here want to work for so little."

"The pay isn't that bad."

"Yes, it is, and you know it."

I studied him for a moment. "Can I tell you something?"

He leaned against the lip of the display case. Herbert had wrinkled cheeks and a bony chin. "Sure can, Miss Tarryn."

"I just—" I glanced around the store. One shopper stood in the small frozen food section, and Marlena maintained her post at the center checkout. "It seems a lot worse since the last time I was here. This town, I mean. Allen was always a little sleepy, but this—this is different."

"I know it is." He nodded a few times. "You feel it, don't you?"

I shrugged. "This whole place just feels... *depressed.* Like there's a thick dust that covers everything."

Herbert's mouth fell into a hard line and he crossed his arms. "Turns out hard times don't get better with age."

"No, they don't. And I also think people have been avoiding their real feelings about the... the—"

"We don't like to talk about it, you know." He raised a hand. "Not one of us. No one from Allen. Too much pain."

"But don't you think you eventually have to? That you have to face it?" I frowned. "That you have to grieve?"

"We've done plenty of that, but there's no easy way to mourn a bunch of innocent dead school kids. No easy way at all. You don't move on from something like that."

I gulped. I knew that. The tragedy of December 13th still dominated the town, even over five years later. A slew of killed children. Logan Powell, behind the wheel of the car that hit the bus, dead too. A school bus driver with a career-ending head injury.

It was the incident that shattered a whole community and changed its course forever.

"Dad told me people wanted him to charge Reid Powell," I whispered. "Back then, they wanted it a lot."

Herbert's face fell further. "People needed someone to blame. And since he survived in one of the other cars, he was the likeliest target. Reid bailed his brother out plenty of times before, always made excuses for him, always covered for Logan's bad behavior. Folks figured he had some responsibility that day too."

"Dad didn't want me to come up here after that." I shuddered. "He said it was too sad, too much. He wasn't... I don't know. I was about to finish high school, and he wanted me to focus on my life in Cincinnati."

"He's very proud of you," Herbert replied. "He told everyone in town when you got that scholarship. Couldn't have been prouder to say his daughter was a Buckeye who had brains."

I leaned against the strawberry display case. "He was never the same after that accident. It aged him."

"People were mad at your father; I'll tell you that. And honestly, they're still mad. Maybe not at him, but it's complicated." Herbert glanced over his shoulder. The lone customer still shopped in the store but had moved to fresh meats and cheeses. He moved closer to me, and his next words came out softer than my own. "Sometimes, people don't want the law. They want vengeance."

"I remember when Dad told me he couldn't prosecute Reid. He didn't have a case. Reid might have been there, but he wasn't the one driving the vehicle that caused the chain reaction."

"If their granddaddy saw what those Powell boys turned into"—Herbert spread a calloused hand— "he'd be ashamed."

I nodded. Herbert's words fit with what I knew about the once-proud family. "Dad said Reid left town for a while after the funerals. After all the publicity."

"Only for a few months. Then he was back, like a lost puppy dog." Herbert sneered. "He sold the old mansion to the city for a third of its worth, and then moved out of town, but not far enough away."

I frowned. "Dad didn't tell me about that."

"He lives just off the state highway, on Springhill Lane. Guess there was an old farmhouse on some family property." Herbert rubbed his hand across the rough stubble of his beard. "We all know he's here. Almost as if we can smell him, even though he mostly keeps to himself."

"He's out on Springhill?" My eyes widened, and my mouth fell open. "You're kidding."

"Wouldn't joke about something like that." Herbert's grimaced. "Honestly, I wish he'd go away for good. We don't want him around here, and we never will."

For the rest of the day, I couldn't stop thinking about my conversation with Herbert. When I arrived home, I knew I had to ask my dad about it. He'd have answers to my burning questions.

I found Dad in the living room, seated in his wheelchair in front of a squawking stream of cable news.

"Glad to see you're feeling better." I placed my keys in the tray by the door, hung my coat on the hook nearby, and wandered into the large front room. "This is a good sign. A really good one."

He smiled as I walked over to kiss him on the cheek. "Things... looking... up..." He spoke out of the stronger side of his mouth.

"Even if the world isn't." I pecked both his cheeks.

"H-how was... work?"

With a sigh, I sat in the plush recliner across from him. My feet were tired, and I knew I'd have to massage the arches before I went to bed. "Good. Not much to do there, so it's easy."

Dad raised a trembling hand. "You... you... you... could go back to... school."

"No. How many times have I told you? I'm your daughter and taking care of you is a priority. I can't imagine something more important than that."

"I have... Nora."

"She's *still* not me. Besides, this is our chance for some quality time." I smiled at him. "Don't you want that, considering we haven't seen each other much over the last several years?"

The muscles on the left side of his face fell. "My fault."

"Don't be silly." I glanced at the large TV. A panel of well-dressed TV anchors argued about global reaction to the latest round of social media posts from the White House. I didn't like that Dad kept the cable news on for hours each day, but I'd given up trying to change the habit. He thought it kept him engaged, and I supposed that was good enough. Anything to keep him from feeling depressed about his current state. "If you want me to leave, all you have to do is keep getting healthier."

He laughed.

"Hey, I'm serious." I put up my hands. "That last doctor appointment was encouraging. They like how stubborn you are, it's an advantage in a situation like this."

I had been surprised at the confidence of Dad's doctor the previous week. He'd explained how in the first three months, Dad's brain was in a heightened state of plasticity, meaning it was capable of healing at a rapid rate. Most of the rehab exercises focused on repetition that would activate neuroplasticity and rewire his brain to control his movement better. It helped knowing that when encouraging Dad to do his exercises. It was also why I understood Dad's obsession with the news and game shows. He wanted *his* brain back.

I folded my hands in my lap and took a deep breath. "By the way, I wanted to ask you something." I turned my attention away from endless analysis on the screen. "Whatever happened to Reid Powell?"

"*Reid Powell?*" Dad frowned and drank some water from the bottle located in a cupholder attached to the wheelchair. "What... made... you... think... think about him?"

"Nothing." I shrugged, hoping to appear nonchalant. "I guess earlier, I was just reflecting on the past."

"D-don't."

"I heard he moved back to town in the last few years or so. After all that happened..." I made a sweeping gesture with my hand. Dad could guess what I meant. "They say that's he's out on one of the few properties the Powells still own."

"Yes... Springhill... Lane."

"Do you ever think about him? Ever wonder if he's okay?"

Dad shook his head.

Then, he shot me half of a wry smile. I'd seen that expression many times before, and it always meant that he wanted to change the subject.

But I wasn't satisfied. I wanted to know more. *Needed* to know more. Something about Reid's story drew me to him, especially now that I was sure *he* lived in the house tucked in the woods off Springhill Lane. For a guy whose family had been synonymous with Allen for years, he lived as a recluse. In exile on the fringe of the town he called home.

How long was this town going to punish him for the sins of his brother?

Dad inhaled a large breath. "Reid Powell... must... live with... himself. Punishment enough."

CHAPTER SIX

Reid

S now was coming. Again.

He smelled it. Felt it in his bones. Tasted it in his mouth. Living in Northeastern Ohio for most of his life had given him the extra sense for a winter storm, and he was never wrong. Snow was coming, and it would be bad. *Blizzard* bad. At least a foot, maybe more, and he guessed it would be the heavy flakes, the sort that weighed down everything and paralyzed life.

Once the precipitation fell, he'd be snowbound in the house until the roads cleared.

Reid let out a low curse before he pulled on his heavy boots and zipped himself into his puffer coat. He had to go to town to get supplies, and he couldn't avoid it. More than anything, he needed ice melt and bottled water. He'd ordered both online, but an email said the order had been delayed.

"So much for two-day shipping," he muttered.

The reality left him with few choices. He could go to Allen and get what he needed or drive to Stansview, the next town over. Any other day, he might have made the trek, but Stansview was even smaller than Allen, and might not have enough salt for the property.

So, Allen it was.

He got in his truck and drove into the village. It was early morning, and the sun would come up soon, but the community had already started to bustle with what counted as life. A few people sat in booths in the diner across from Country Market, and a half dozen cars rimmed the Victor County Courthouse square. He parked the truck near the grocery store front door and surveyed the salesfloor through windows painted with the latest specials on meat and cheese. To his surprise, no one shopped inside. He didn't see Marlena on the floor, either.

Better go now while you still can.

He hopped out of the cab, locked the truck, grabbed a cart from the outside carousel, and slipped through the doors. Reid knew the general layout of the store well, and he walked over to the housewares section first. Three dozen or so bags of ice melt were stacked on the bottom metal shelves. He took four of them.

Still alone in the aisles, he pushed the cart to the rows of bottled water. Stock there ran low too. He grabbed two cases of a dozen each. Maybe that would be enough. Maybe not. He couldn't be sure, and if the pipes froze, those bottles might be his only source of fresh water. However, he wouldn't clean out the store's supply.

Others might need it.

The water went on top of the salt in the cart, and he decided he'd traverse the aisles one more time, in case anything else he might need came to mind. Then, he'd leave before the rest of Allen realized the severity of the incoming storm and rushed the store for extra supplies.

Reid turned down the center row and browsed the lines of canned goods, staring at the labels in a sort of daze. Truth was, he relished this moment, of being alone in public, in a place he only frequented when he had to. It was nice, and—

"Reid Powell?" a man's voice screeched. "Reid *fucking* Powell? Oh shit, it's you."

Reid looked up to find a burly, brusque man in an auto mechanic jumpsuit, unzipped barn jacket, hat, and gloves. Frank Watson. Once a childhood friend.

Reid's reply came out stiff and pointed. "Nice to see you, Frank."

"What the hell are you doing here?" Frank glared at him, an expression filled with anger and hatred, a clear indicator that he didn't feel the same about seeing Reid. "Of all the goddamn places."

"I'm shopping. Like you." Reid nodded at the can Frank held in his hand. "Storm's coming our way."

Frank glanced at the wide store windows. "Doesn't look like that to me. Crystal clear outside."

"It's coming."

Frank turned back to Reid. "How would you know? Got a crystal ball or something?"

"I feel it." Reid sighed, then tried to hide it. He just wanted to leave and wanted to end this conversation.

Frank had a beef with him. And more than enough reason to feel that way.

"If you'll excuse me." He maneuvered the cart and tried to step around Frank. Maybe this would end right then, with no other words exchanged between the two men. "I should pay for these."

Frank blocked the pathway in front of the cart. "Maybe you shouldn't." He nodded at the housewares section. "Why don't you put that ice melt back, leave some for people who need it. People who have to *work* for a living."

Reid regarded his former friend. He'd expected this from Frank, just like he did from everyone, but the reality of it still stung like one of the sharp switches his mother swatted him with during his worst childhood punishments. "No, I don't think I'm going to do that."

"Well, I suggest that you do." Frank put two hands on Reid's cart and thrust the full weight of his body forward. "But on second thought, I can see you're still a selfish bastard. Just like the rest of your bloodline."

Reid had a thousand replies. He chose none of them.

"Jennifer's birthday was last week," Frank added under his breath. "Did you think about her? She would have been eleven. In the fifth grade, for Christ's sake."

Reid winced at the sound of Jennifer's name. *Crack.* Another sharp pain shot through him. "I know."

Of course, he knew. He *always* knew. The last few years had been full of moments like that, strands of "would haves" and "should haves," all of which had turned into "nevers." Jennifer would never start high school. Or turn sixteen. Or graduate. Or have a first kiss. Or…

"Do you even think about her? Remember my daughter at all?" Frank narrowed his eyes. "No, I don't believe so."

"I think about her all the time. Not as much as you, but a lot." Reid's shoulders slumped, and a heaviness grew around him, as it always did whenever someone mentioned Jennifer, Kelly, Melissa, Brent... and the other children killed that horrible day. Reid shut his eyes and tried to sweep them from his mind. It didn't work. "I didn't forget her. I'll *never* forget her."

"Bullshit."

Reid opened his eyes and set his jaw. Bullshit? It wasn't that. Not even close. For a second, he wanted to swing right at Frank, but Reid didn't have the energy or the mood to argue with someone who'd suffered such a huge loss. Frank had the upper hand there and carried pain three times the size of Reid's. No matter what, the loss of Jennifer would be with him forever. Frank would win this fight.

Instead, Reid pushed his shopping cart away, as if the handle was as hot as an oven range. "Know what? I don't need this stuff anymore. I forgot that I had an extra supply in the garage. You take it, it's yours." He nodded at the man he'd once rode a bus with to school, and who'd been his fellow Cub Scout. "Have a good day, Frank."

He'd get what he needed another way. Without another word, Reid strode out of the grocery store and into the cold.

47

Tarryn

"Did you hear about the storm, Miss Tarryn?" Herbert asked when I walked into the Country Market stockroom that evening. It was just after eight, and the store would close soon.

"Oh, yeah, of course. We've been busy all night. Everybody is talking about it."

And buying all the milk we had. The eggs. The bread.

"Have you seen this?" Herbert showed me the doppler radar app on his phone and let out a low whistle. "Look at that."

"Oh, man, that system is a monster. Bigger than I thought."

Herbert put his phone in his back pocket. "The news alert said it's getting worse with every mile. That snow from Canada, once it crosses the Great Lakes..." He nodded to himself. "First real blizzard of the season."

"They didn't predict this one very well."

"What did you expect? Local news. Those meteorologists are nothing but weather guessers. I think the girl who anchors the six o'clock show is younger than you." Herbert picked up one of the cardboard boxes Country Market used to fulfill the few delivery orders for the store each week. "Gonna have to get these deliveries out before the snow hits."

"How long do we have until the worst of it is here?" I glanced at the foggy windows that lined the far wall of the stockroom. You couldn't guess just from looking through those. Winter darkness coated the panes, reducing visibility.

"Two hours. Maybe three. Moving pretty fast now that it's picked up speed across Lake Erie."

I pointed at the stack of already filled orders. "And you still need to deliver these?"

"Yep."

"Why don't you let me help you?" I picked up the clipboard on the cardboard table next to the orders. Fifteen or so needed fulfillment by the end of the day. "Marlena has the store covered, and I don't have much to do." I flipped the pages that outlined the customers' needs. "This won't take long."

"You think Marlena will mind?"

"No. She said the other day that I was welcome to do deliveries, if I wanted to."

"Well, thank you. That's mighty kind of you, Miss Tarryn."

I read the orders again, and my eyes fell to the last name on the list. Reid Powell. An order of five bags of salt and two twelve packs of bottled water. "Hmm."

"Hmm, what?"

I looked up from the clipboard and gave Herbert a tight smile. "Nothing." I turned the clipboard in his direction. "What do you say we divide these orders up? You deliver the top half, and I'll do the bottom? Won't take as long if we do it that way."

"Good idea." Herbert took three empty boxes from the pile nearest him. He passed them to me. "Let's hop to it."

CHAPTER SEVEN

Tarryn

T he work took longer than expected, and we finished packing the orders just as snow began to fall.

Oversized, sweeping, wet flakes dusted the
sidewalks, the road, and the cars outside. It added to the
inch-wide layer of snow that often arrived during late fall
and lingered until after Easter. It mingled with the strag-
gled icicles that hung from gutters and rooftops. The snow
coated everything in a deceiving calm.

"Look at that. The news got it wrong again. It came
early," Herbert said.

"Have to admit, it looks beautiful." I placed the final
order into the back of my car.

"That's only until it turns into gray slush." Herbert
rubbed his mittens together then crossed his arms. "Whew,
temperature is really dropping."

"We should get these out." I opened the driver's side door. Snow already stuck to my hair and clung to my eyelashes. "Can't afford to delay."

"Are you sure you want to do this?"

"It's only seven houses. I can make it in half an hour."

"But—"

"No buts. Don't overthink this." I clapped a gloved hand on the rubber that rimmed the car door window. "People need these supplies if there's going to be a blizzard. We can't let them down."

"That's true." Herbert surveyed the dark sky as if he was going to find another argument, then brought his attention back to me. "Still, look at how fast this is falling."

He was right, and the streetlight over his left shoulder illuminated his point. The flakes had a nice clip to them. A purpose. When it was done, this storm would claim everything in the valley.

"Then let's go. No time to waste," I told him. "I'll call the store when I'm done if that will make you feel better about it."

"You win, then." He smiled. "And I probably should know better than to argue with the daughter of our prosecutor."

In the next few minutes I was in the car, and out making deliveries.

I saved Reid's order for last. Logically, this didn't make sense. I should have dropped his order off first, then worked through the remaining addresses as they brought me closer to my dad's house. That would have put me home safely. But I couldn't stop thinking about Reid Powell, and I wanted to save that curiosity for last, like a treat for finishing my other work.

What was he like? Did he enjoy shutting himself off? Was he lonely?

The trip to Reid's address came just before nine thirty, and when the storm had already dumped a solid half inch of powder on Allen and the farmland that rimmed the community.

"Delivery from Country Market," I said into the farmhouse front door as I knocked a few times. In front of the entrance was a ragged woven rug, and I wiped my thick winter boots on it. The wood planks on the front porch appeared to have a fresh coat of paint, though, and a small wreath hung from the door. I waited about ninety seconds then rapped again. "Is anyone home?"

The door flung open seconds later. The force of it caught me off guard, and a small yelp escaped my lips.

"Oh, hi," I managed. "How are you? Um... so... here's the stuff that you wanted."

Reid stood on the other side of the door with wide eyes and a cocked head. He wore a red plaid flannel shirt and a pair of dark jeans. His hair was shorter than the last time I saw him, but the dark stubble still framed his jaw and contrasted with his brilliant blue eyes. Those could have been sapphires, and they sat deep in his face underneath thick brows and a wide forehead.

"Thank you for the delivery." His words were stiff and wooden. "Thank you very much."

He took the box from me and placed it behind the front door. When he bent at the waist, I noticed how his back flowed into his hips like a tapered V. I couldn't help myself—but I didn't want to *un-see* it, either.

Oh, wow, this man is gorgeous.

The thought traveled across my mind like a breaking news alert.

We stared at each other. Rather, *I* stared at *him*. How could I not? Despite his rough exterior, there was something soft and almost broken about this person. It all made him look less like a mountain man, and more like simply a man.

"Do you have the other part of the order?" he asked after a moment.

"Yes." I stumbled backward again as if his words had thrown me off my axis. "I mean… sure. It's in the trunk." I moved farther away. "I'm—let me get it." I pushed off the steps and returned to the Camry's trunk, which I heaved open. "It's right—"

But he was already down the front steps too, and out in the snow with no coat, hat, or gloves. He reached the car and grabbed the side of a pack of water.

"I've got it," he mumbled.

"I do too."

Together, we moved the water from the car to the house. The whole thing took less than two minutes.

"Hold on," he said as I brushed my hands on my jeans. Reid pushed through the front door and disappeared into the house. When he returned, he had five dollars in his hand. "For your trouble tonight."

"Thanks." I took the money and shoved it in my coat pocket. He was the only customer that night to offer me anything extra for my delivery, and it was kind of him to make the gesture. "So, um…" I held out my hand. I was doing anything to extend this limited interaction. "I should probably introduce myself. I'm Tarryn Long."

"I'm Reid Powell. And I know who you are." He shook my hand, and all I saw were his wide, patrician fingers.

"How?"

"Because it's Allen. Someone new shows up—everyone knows about it. And besides, you're Peter Long's daughter, aren't you?" There was a heaviness in his last sentence, and sadness pulled at his eyes.

"Yes." I bit my bottom lip.

We stared at each other for a beat before he pointed at the packs of water. "So, you're working at Country Market." He put his hands in the back pockets of his jeans. If the cold bothered him, it didn't register on his weary face. "I assume, since you made this run out to my place."

"Part-time. I took a semester off from Ohio State and moved here to take care of Dad after he had the stroke."

"Heard about that. How is he?"

Once again came the usual line of questioning. "Better than expected," I replied, giving a vague, bland answer. It was all most people wanted to hear.

"Sorry about what happened to him."

"Thanks." A nervous pang rushed through me, and I looked down at the porch slats. "He says I shouldn't have moved here. That he could have recovered on his own."

"But you came anyway."

I met his gaze. "I figured a few months couldn't hurt. It's not that much to make up. I'll get my marketing degree soon enough."

A beat passed. "And do you like it here?"

"Do you?"

"No one really likes Allen." He let out a hollow laugh. "But we all stay regardless."

"Why?"

"Because it's home. And I... well, that's what it is. Home."

It was the answer everyone gave me, a refrain that echoed through the entire valley. And for whatever reason, I shuddered. It wasn't just what they were saying, it was the *way* they said it. As if living here wasn't a choice.

"So here you are, on this property at the edge of town, all alone," I said to fill the space between us. "By yourself."

"Since you're Peter Long's daughter, I'm sure you know why." His gaze bored into me. His jaw was set. His expression almost blank.

And he was right. I did.

"I should go," I said because I couldn't think of anything else to say, and I wasn't sure I wanted to pry into all the awful details of the accident. But despite the horrible way the people of Allen treated him, I wondered why he was so alone. If I'd learned anything from my parents' divorce was that there were always two sides to each story. From what Herbert said, even my dad had borne the weight of what happened, and I knew he hadn't deserved that. What if Reid wasn't the monster he was thought to be? *He lives alone. He wants solitude. He doesn't need friends. Just leave.*

I sighed and surveyed the distance between his front porch and the car. Twenty feet, maybe a few more. Already covered in flakes heavy enough to make our tracks disappear. "How many inches do you think we'll get?"

"At least fifteen before it's over. Maybe closer to twenty."

I recoiled. "They didn't say that much on the news."

"They don't know what they're talking about."

"Well," I said, wishing I had something else to say to him. "I suppose I really *should* go, then."

"Absolutely." He jerked his chin in the direction of my Camry. "But are you sure a car like that can make it home?"

"It's never failed me before. Okay, well, goodbye." I took another deep breath, gave myself another look at him, and turned on my booted heels.

When I got to the car, he still stood in the doorway, watching me. The snow nearly covered the front windshield. And as I backed out of the driveway, I couldn't help but feel an extra chill in my bones.

CHAPTER EIGHT

Reid

H e heard the crash less than two minutes after he closed the front door. Broken metal. Shattering glass. A screech that pierced the night.

Damn it. I shouldn't have let her drive.

Reid took his coat from the front closet, wrapped a scarf around his neck, and pushed the hat on his head, and raced out into the storm. He should have offered to at least help her get to the highway, which he knew would be clearer than winding Springhill Lane. He'd even considered it as she stood on the porch. The storm was bad, the snowflakes more powerful than they looked. The wind howled through the trees. Add in the frigid temperatures, and it brewed together like a thick stew.

He followed the tracks down the driveway, drawing closer to the blinking brake lights a few dozen feet from where his property connected with the highway, and the rest of civilization. Dread grew with each frantic step.

I'll never forgive myself if she got hurt...

The car had slid off the dirt road, and into a tree. The front bumper wound around the trunk like a messy Band-Aid, and the left headlight blinked lazily. The right headlight lay in shards of plastic on the snow.

Tarryn sat in the front seat. She didn't look injured. Music still played on the car stereo, providing a bizarre soundtrack to the moment.

"What a mess," he said when he reached the driver's side door. He took stock of her and was relieved she didn't have any visible wounds. "You okay?"

Wincing, she massaged her neck. "Guess so. My head is starting to throb."

"Looks like you hit the tree pretty hard."

"I just slid right into it."

"You could have been seriously hurt. That crash sure sounded like you were." He exhaled. "I shouldn't have placed that order tonight. I shouldn't have forced you to come out here. That was my mistake."

"I wanted to make the delivery. You needed the supplies, after all."

"Ice melt won't do much good on a night like this any way, and I was stupid to think that it would. Better to just hunker down and—" He narrowed his eyes. "You're still pulling on your neck. Are you sure you're fine?"

"Yes. No... I don't... I don't know. I think I hit some ice underneath the snow. Not totally sure how it happened, but I lost control." She regarded the twisted car parts and half folded front end. "I tensed up there for a moment."

Reid looked over at the intersection of Springhill Lane and the highway. Just as he suspected. Thick snow blanketed both directions and blended the trees with the road. No tire ruts. No sign of a snow plow. No sign of life at all.

"Bad news." He braced one hand on hood. "The weather is getting too awful. You won't be able to get a tow truck tonight." He glanced at her car. "And you certainly can't drive this thing."

"Don't you think we should at least try to get help?" She picked up her phone from the console. "There has to be someone out on the streets from Triple A."

He shook his head. "They won't come this way. Not like this." He brushed some snow from his shoulders and ignored the dropping temperature. "There's already at least two inches of snow. Maybe more than that. The crews won't clear it until it stops falling."

"I don't want to leave my car here." She threw up a hand. "I was just trying—"

"To do your job."

She sighed. "Yes. And now my car's a wreck."

He looked at the tangled metal again. "You'll have to leave it here."

"How am I going to get home?"

"Come on," he replied. "Let's get back to the house. I've got some aspirin, and my truck has snow tires. We'll see if that can make it. Better than nothing, right?"

Tarryn stared at him a few breaths, then nodded in agreement. After she turned off the sedan, they trudged in silence back up the long lane toward his property. The snow crunched around them, and the wind lashed their faces. Still, he marveled at how good it felt to interact with someone different, someone other than the people he paid to help him take care of what remained of the Powell legacy. Someone with wavy blonde hair, and a light in her eyes...

By the time they arrived back at the house, the falling snow had already wiped away the tire ruts her car had made. They dashed up the porch stairs, and he found aspirin in the first-floor bathroom.

He brought her two caplets and a glass of water. "Not much, but it's a start. You should probably get your neck checked out tomorrow."

"Thanks for these." She swallowed the medicine without taking a drink. "I can't believe how bad it is out there. My car's going to be covered in the next hour."

"Winter in Allen. Might as well be the North Pole."

She laughed at his joke, and he studied her again as they stood in the foyer. She was beautiful, but in a slightly unconventional way. Aside from her thick blonde hair, Tarryn had eyes as round and as deep as blue topaz jewels. Three moles dotted her left cheek, and one was just above her lip, which she'd outlined with maroon lipstick. Tarryn was also thin, but her heavy coat outlined curvy hips.

Reid realized once again she was a woman unmarked by the hard living so unmistakable in the people around Allen.

Something twitched in his stomach, then between his legs. He hadn't felt a sensation like that in so long, he almost didn't recognize it. Even more, he wondered if he'd feel it every time he was around her.

Reid cleared his throat, trying to shake off his obvious attraction to her. *Focus, man. Focus.* "If we don't get going soon, the storm will be too much, even for my truck."

"Of course."

He zipped his coat tighter and moved around her to leave, but she caught his arm. He noticed her chipped red nails, a thin necklace around her neck, and a small silver ring on her middle finger.

"Thanks, Reid. You've really helped me tonight."

His breath hitched. Something stirred deep inside him when she said his name, something he hadn't felt in a long time. Something that made him wonder if she was someone different, someone who saw him as a real person—

"You're welcome. Least I can do."

Reid pulled away from her and burst out onto the front porch again, knowing she'd follow him. No need to lock the front door. No one came to see him anyway, and the snow would give the house an extra layer of protection. He stomped down the steps toward his truck, pushing through the snow, feeling her behind him. By the time he reached the vehicle, every cell in his body was aware of Tarryn.

Is this what being awake feels like?

"Get in," he muttered. If he brought his eyes to hers, he'd stare too hard, so he kept his face down, his gaze away. "It's unlocked."

"Okay—"

"Hurry."

The reply came out too sharp and jagged, and he knew that, but he couldn't stop himself. Reid didn't interact with many people, so he was rusty on the finer points of conversation. He didn't know how to be soft, how to be rounded instead of pointed. He didn't know how to open the gates around his soul.

They slid into the front seat, and he turned on the headlights. The snow was close to blinding, and the lights showed off the thick, heavy precipitation. Getting her home would be a challenge, but he'd do it anyway. She'd gone out of her way to make sure he had supplies, and he could do the same for her.

Reid shoved the key into the ignition. He turned it. The engine sputtered. Then died. He cranked it again. Another sputter.

"Shit." He slammed his palms on the steering wheel. "*Shit.*"

"What is it?"

He allowed himself to look at her. "I think it's the battery."

Her jaw went slack. "Can you jump it?"

"Yes." He turned his head toward the garage. "I can jump it. But I don't know—"

"I need to get home. I can't…" She grabbed the handle on the passenger door. Her voice grew agitated. "It's getting late, and my dad—"

"Don't worry. I've got it."

He leapt out of the truck and into the snow again. *Fix this, Reid. Fix it now.* He stored jumper cables in the garage next to the lawnmower alongside a battery charger, but when he fixed it all to the dead one, the engine still didn't engage.

"Damn," he yelled. "Damn."

She got out of his truck, hunched her shoulders, and her hands went deep into her coat pockets. "Not working, huh?"

He shook his head.

She looked out at the falling snow, and the cold blanket it created over the property. "It's getting worse."

"Like I said earlier."

"We have to find some way to get me home." She shivered. "I can't…"

Reid sighed and closed the hood. He knew this storm, he felt it in his bones. "Even if we get the truck started, the weather is too bad. The flakes are coming down too hard."

It was an obvious statement, but he made it anyway.

"Come on." He jerked his head at the house. "You can stay the night. Can you call someone to be with your dad? I'm really sorry, Tarryn." *Sorrier than she'll ever know.*

CHAPTER NINE

Tarryn

Getting snowed in with Reid Powell wasn't the *worst* thing that could have happened. I had to admit that. Even though I barely knew him, I was warm, inside, and safe as the storm outside turned into a full blizzard. And it gave me a chance to scratch my curiosity, which grew stronger by the moment.

"Thanks again for all the help," I said from my place at the kitchen table as he handed me a cup of coffee spiked with a shot or so of Bailey's Irish Cream. After giving up on the car for the night, he'd suggested the drink. I sipped some of the steaming liquid. "Oh, that's nice."

"Like a hug in a mug."

"A strong one."

"After the last two hours, we deserve it."

"You're right." I placed the cup on the pockmarked wood table. It fit with the rustic décor of the kitchen, which included a gas stove, a smattering of ancient iron pans hanging on the wall, and a gleaming white sink. "I keep thinking about the car, and what a mess that's going to be in the morning."

"The crash did at least a few thousand dollars' worth of damage to it." Clutching his own mug, he sat across from me at the table. "We'll call a tow truck first thing in the morning."

"Speaking of which"—I snapped my fingers— "I'll text my dad."

"Will he be okay without you there tonight?"

"Sometimes Nora stays overnight, so I'm going to tell her what's going on."

I picked up my phone from the table and typed out several quick messages telling them both I'd had an accident, I was safe, and I'd be back in the morning once the roads were cleared. As I finished the messages, I raised my head and looked at Reid again. "So… umm… do you think I should I tell them I'm staying with *you*?"

"You can if you want."

"I can only imagine the look on Dad's face when he gets the message."

Reid's nostrils flared. "He won't like that."

"Because of the case? Because of your brother and what happened?" I felt awful coming at Reid with little filter, but it was as though some part of me needed to know his story. I was overstepping boundaries here, but I'd probably never get the chance again to talk to him about it again. *He lost in that accident too.*

"The town may be small, but their memories are anything but." He pointed at my phone and my unsent text message. "No, I wouldn't tell him you're with me."

He had a point. My father had gone through a lot in the last few months, and he hadn't been happy when I'd mentioned Reid the other day. If Dad truly hated him, then getting a message that I was spending the night with him would only upset him. So, I added one white lie to the text.

"There," I said after I hit send on the last message. "I told him I'm with Herbert from the store. He won't question that one."

"Herbert Scofield is harmless." Reid drank some more of his spiked coffee. He was right. Brusque, yet right.

We shared a long silence as the night grew darker and the storm intensified. After a while, Reid got up from the table and walked into the living room. "Just realized how cold it is in here," he called over his shoulder. "I'll make a fire."

"I can help." I followed him.

"No, I've got it." He was already at the other end of the room, holding a large piece of fire wood.

I sank into the couch and allowed myself a few quiet moments to study Reid. He was thin where it mattered and sculpted where it didn't, a strange mix of strength and fragility I hadn't seen in any of the guys on campus at Ohio State. He was all man, fully formed, and sure of himself. As I watched, Reid made quick, deft work of the fire, and within a few moments, it warmed the large living room.

"There," he said as he brushed his hands on the sides of his jeans. "That should work."

"Very impressive." I watched him as he proudly crossed the room to the chair that matched the sofa. "That was practically textbook."

He sat. "Just learned it over the years. My father took us camping when my brother and I were young."

"I guess those are good skills for man who likes to live alone."

His eyes narrowed, and the light inside them faded, making me immediately regret my off-handed comment.

"I mean, I don't know if you *like* it—"

"That depends on the day, I guess," he said, then focused on the fire again. The embers crackled, and the flames grew as the heat took over the wood. The implication of his last two words hung between us. Of course he was lonely. He had to be.

"Have you ever thought about... I don't know... about trying to win them over?" I cleared my throat. Talking to him inevitably meant also talking about *it*. Them. That moment. "I mean the people of Allen? They must forgive you at some point. You didn't do anything, and—"

"That's the point. I didn't do *anything*, Tarryn." Reid crossed his arms. "It's my fault that those kids died in the accident that day. Those families don't have their children at home tonight."

"But wasn't your brother an adult? Isn't he responsible for what—?"

"No." Reid's hand sliced the air. "It wasn't like that. You weren't there, anyway. You don't know."

"I just—"

"It's not something I like to talk about. Especially with strangers."

I stared at him. Yes, I was a stranger, but his words still hurt me. He was so closed off; it was almost like he had a thick shell around him. How could anyone want to live this way, alone, and permanently separated from the town they called home? It didn't make sense.

"You can talk about it to me," I tried. "I'll listen."

Reid raised an eyebrow and looked away from me. "All I will say is, on the day of the accident, I wanted to stop Logan. But I was too late."

"All of this guilt is like a prison," I murmured. "One that you put yourself in."

"I assure you, it's not the jail you think it is." Reid stood from the chair. "It's late. I should probably show you to your room."

Without another word, he led up me a winding staircase to the second floor. We passed two bedrooms and a small second bathroom before he opened a door at the end of the hall. A queen-sized bed, desk, and bureau awaited me.

"It's not much," he said as I stepped into the room.

"No, it's great." I turned around to face him. I wasn't sure what I expected to see in his face, but the curiosity in his expression surprised me. "Thank you."

"For what?" Reid braced his arm on the door frame.

"All of this." I gestured to the bed. "For not leaving me out in the cold. For offering me a place to stay during a blizzard."

"I might be a monster," he replied. "But I'm not heartless."

And then, he was gone.

Reid

Human connection—*real* human connection—might as well have been a foreign language to him. He was rusty, like the grinding gears on an old bike, and he knew that with every cell in his body. In fact, he still considered himself *less* than human, but having a woman in his home, and another person to talk to during the long, lonely hours, was more welcome than he'd expected. By the time he arrived at the master bedroom on the first floor of the house, goosebumps checkered his arms and sweat beaded on his neck.

He tossed himself onto the antique bed and stared at the ceiling. She was above him in the room on the second floor, and he focused on the fine cracks in the plaster as he allowed his thoughts to drift to her.

Tarryn Long.

Tarryn Long. Tarryn Long. *Tarryn Long*...

He liked the way her name sounded when he said it in his mind, the same way he liked the curves of her body, the point of her nose, and the way she'd shown him a few glimpses of stubbornness that came with being a prosecutor's daughter. He had to admit, he didn't mind the snow so much anymore, because it had brought her along with it.

You can't get too close, Reid. You know that. People who get close to you get burned.

But it felt good—nice even, to have someone in the house along with him. His self-imposed confinement had always seemed like the best option, the clearest way to punish himself for his personal failings, but it had also come with plenty of sidebar costs. Loneliness wasn't a dream. Many days, it was a nightmare.

After a few moments, he stripped off his clothes, found pajamas in the closet, and climbed underneath the bedcovers. He was tired and wary, but it wasn't just because winter had settled in all around him. Life had become mundane, and boring.

What if he could have something else, something other than enforced solitude? Tarryn's presence had caused a ripple in his daily punishment. It had also highlighted a need deep within his bones. What if he actually wanted something more?

That was all he could think about as he drifted to sleep.

CHAPTER TEN

Reid

W hen he awoke the next morning, the bedclothes twisted around his body and sweat drenched his sheets. It was just after six, and darkness still coated the outdoors. He walked to the window and assessed the snow. By his estimate, at least fourteen inches had fallen during the night. Maybe more.

Shit.

They wouldn't get off the property that morning—if at all that day. He'd have to clear the snow piles first, and that would take hours, even with the large plow he kept in the garage.

Then we'll have to dig out Tarryn's car…

He threw on some clothes then walked from the bedroom to the kitchen, wondering how he'd break it to her. He didn't have a good answer for that question, so he decided he'd make some breakfast. Eggs and coffee might go a long way toward softening the blow that would come from hearing she had to spend more time with him.

Reid opened the fridge and took out the egg carton. He found the coffee in the cabinet and took one of the cast iron skillets from the wall. He almost dropped it to the floor.

Tarryn stood in the doorway, staring at him.

"Didn't see you there," he said. "You startled me."

"Sorry about that. I just woke up." She rubbed her eyes. Her hair was rumpled, and eye makeup smeared her cheeks. She still wore the previous day's clothes, but they had new wrinkles and creases. "And before I came down here, I looked outside. It's not good."

"This storm was one for the books." He put the skillet on the table. "Haven't seen something like this in the valley in at least a decade."

"How am I going to get home? I can't stay here." She leaned against the door frame and folded her arms. "I have to get back and—"

He jerked his head at the window. "But you're not going outside right now. It's too dangerous. Besides, it's not like you'll stay here forever. This isn't a prison."

"No, it's just yours."

He stiffened and turned back to the breakfast. "You know, you're lucky you're here," he said as he cracked an egg on the side of the skillet. "You could be out there, having spent the night in the car." He dumped the gooey yolk into the pan, then followed it with two more. "Out there freezing. I'm the one who rescued *you*, remember?"

"You're right. I'm sorry if I sounded ungrateful. I'm just worried about my dad, since this storm was worse than we expected," she replied. He heard her move to the kitchen table and take a seat. "I'm thankful you helped me last night. Waking up here was certainly better than waking up out there."

He added heat to the range and faced her. "Listen, I'm rusty at this. I don't talk to a lot of people."

"Apology accepted. Can we start again?"

Start again…

"Yes." He swallowed the lump in his throat. How much he wanted to start *everything* in life again. "We can."

"Okay. Good morning, Reid Powell."

"Good morning, Tarryn Long. I hope you had a good sleep, because I have bad news about the storm."

"Oh, no, what's that?"

"You're probably trapped here at least for the day." He jerked his head at the window over the sink. "It will take a while for me to clear that mess, even with the snowmobile I have in the garage."

"Wow. You're right, that blizzard was bad." She let out a low whistle as she surveyed the land outside. "It's a winter wonderland out there."

"So, you're stuck with me." The eggs had begun to cook, and he stirred them with the spatula. "Want some breakfast? I'm not a gourmet cook, so I hope you like scrambled eggs."

"It's perfect." She got up from the kitchen table and padded over to him. "What are we having with them?"

He blinked at her. He hadn't thought about that.

"Well…" He walked over to the pantry and flung open the door. "I have"—he pulled out an unopened box of Frosted Flakes— "this."

She laughed. "A sugar rush and some protein. I like it."

He placed the box on the counter. "Perfect, because my other suggestion was Lucky Charms."

"Magically delicious."

They shared a laugh, and he felt something thaw inside his chest. She was warm, inviting, and most of all, not judging him right then for any of the past. That was nice. Refreshing. A way to start again.

"Where can I find the bowls?" Tarryn asked. "If we're going to have a sugar binge, we better do it properly."

Reid pointed her in the direction of the dinnerware, then returned to the eggs. Once their breakfast was ready, they sat across from each other at the wide table. She'd added placemats and his nicest plates, along with the best silverware in his drawer.

"A feast," she commented as she put her napkin in her lap. "All we need are mimosas."

"That would really round out the sugar content."

"On the contrary, you can *never* have enough sugar. Especially if we are going to work on clearing all the snow. We'll burn it right off without trying."

He took a bite of the eggs, wanting to try them before she did. Luckily, they didn't taste burned or too runny. He gave himself a point for that and felt relieved.

"This is good," she said after a few bites of cereal. "I'd forgotten how much I used to love Frosted Flakes. I don't think I've eaten them in years."

Reid took a bite of cereal. "When I was a kid, I liked the Nintendo cereal, Count Chocula, and the one that had Reese's Cups."

"All banned at my mom's house. Totally on the no list. But at my dad's? All I ate were Fruit Loops and Apple Cinnamon Cheerios."

"Your dad has decent taste, then."

"Every once in a while." She bit into some eggs. "By the way, these are yummy. You're a good cook."

"Cooking scrambled eggs doesn't exactly make me a gourmet chef." He smiled. He was enjoying himself. Enjoying this. Here was a beautiful woman sitting across from him, and she was treating him like a normal person, like a human being. For years, only Walter had done that.

Reid continued to eat his eggs but took his time. He wanted to extend this moment, this interaction, if he could. And yet, he knew it would be over before he knew it.

It was.

"So, I'm not going to let you do all the work alone," Tarryn said when they had empty plates and full bellies. "It will take forever if it's just you clearing the snow."

"It will take a few hours, even for the two of us." Reid looked out the kitchen window at the thick blanket of powder outside. "Half the day, maybe."

"We'll probably find my car totally buried and have to dig it out." She stood from the table and picked up the plates. "I'm curious—how do you take care of this place? It's too much for one person."

"I have help." Reid stood and walked over to the sink. Together, they cleaned the plates in the wide basin. "Walter does a lot. He comes here twice a week and does odd jobs. It's more of a loyalty thing than anything else. Walter used to work for the family before—before we lost what we had. And he stayed."

"That's very kind of him."

"It's not what you think." Reid turned off the water and studied her. "He's around because I pay him. That's all."

"But—"

"There's no buts about it, Tarryn. People know who I am. *What* I am." He sharpened his tone of voice. He wanted to make sure she understood his next words. "And it's better if they don't get too close. They need to stay away from me."

Something fell behind her eyes, and he knew he'd confused her. Hurt her, even. He'd closed whatever door had cracked opened during breakfast. *Good.* Exactly the way it needed to be. Tarryn was nice, pretty, and smart. But she didn't need to get too close to him. If the people of Allen knew she associated with him, they'd reject her too. Scorn her. She didn't deserve that.

No. Tarryn Long deserved happiness. The less time she spent here the better. *No matter how much I like her presence.*

She'd only get hurt.

Tarryn

I couldn't figure Reid out.

Not that I was really giving it my best effort, but I was curious. He was such an... enigma. I kept thinking about that as I used the blower to clear the walkway around the porch. Reid drove the truck-sized snowplow a few hundred yards away, and through my peripheral vision, I watched him push the snow off the driveway and into the side yard. It created a huge trench, but at least we were closer to my car, and closer to me leaving.

And part of me *wanted* to leave.

But another part of me didn't.

Who was this man, this person who couldn't seem to forgive himself for past sins? This man who lived in self-imposed exile, not because of something he'd done, but because of something his *brother* did? This man seemed to hate himself.

I pushed the snowblower a bit more, still thinking about what he'd said. *"I didn't do anything, Tarryn. That's the issue... It's my fault those kids died in the accident that day."* Was that true? Was he *really* guilty, like my dad and others had said?

Me and my big mouth. At breakfast, it had felt like I was getting somewhere, as if he'd started to allow me to see a side of himself that had been hidden. The eggs and the cereal had done it; he'd started to give in, to feel human.

But then, he'd closed himself off again. Shut down. Kept himself behind a wall. And now, here we were, clearing snow so I could leave, and he'd continue to keep himself locked away.

What a sad way to live. A sad way to be.

It doesn't have to be like this, does it?

"How much snow do you think you've plowed?" I asked him around noon, when the arduous task of clearing a main pathway through the snow was finally done. We were sweaty and breathing hard as we took in the sight of our efforts from inside the front door. When it came to blizzards, Northeastern Ohio always made sure to make an impression.

"A few hundred feet, maybe? I'm not sure," Reid replied between haggard gasps of air. He took off his thick gloves, ripped off his heavy coat, and wiped his brow. I followed his lead. As cold as it was outside, the inside of the house was as warm. "Hopefully this is the worst of it, but it's only January."

"Long winter ahead."

He nodded. "March always brings her own challenges." He surveyed the property and the large trench that now connected the farmhouse with Springhill Lane, and then with the highway. "The good news is, I was able to get most of the stuff off your car. The tow truck won't have to do too much work in order to dig you out."

"Thank you."

"You're welcome." Not looking at me, he removed his thick work boots and placed them outside on the porch. When he returned, his face had changed again, to an expression I couldn't read. "Well, we should probably call them now, so that you can get home to your dad."

"I'll call them."

It was the only way to reply. Not that Reid was a huge conversationalist, but he seemed reluctant to engage in much conversation after that point. When the tow truck arrived, there was nothing left to say but thank you, to which Reid simply replied, 'You're welcome'. And so, our private time together ended.

Dad and Nora were at the house when I got home. The service towed my damaged car to the mechanic without any problems, but my car needed major repairs. Nora greeted me at the door with a hug then led me to the living room where Dad still sat in front of the TV. Only the channel had changed, from twenty-four-hour news to the local coverage of the storm.

"You said not to worry about you, but we still did," Nora said as I took a seat on the couch. "This was a bad one. Fourteen inches on average fell in the region."

"Wow." I watched a few moments of the endless coverage. A brunette reporter in a thick black jacket and a red beret stood next to an enormous pile of plowed snow, which had turned gray from dirt and dust. "Is that a record? Seems like one."

"It's an amount we haven't seen in a long time."

Dad turned to me in his wheelchair. "Spent... the night at... Herbert's?"

"No, not at his house. Just in the backroom his mother rents." The fake excuse was getting easier to tell. Being with Reid—in any way—needed to remain my little secret. "It was nice."

"She was kind to let you stay there," Nora said.

"She was." My thoughts turned to my wrecked Camry and the sober assessment the mechanic had made about its crumpled state. "What are we going to do about the car?"

"We... can... fix," Dad replied.

"What if it's expensive?"

"Will be okay." He studied me. "At... least not... hurt."

We settled in and watched more of the local news coverage. Nora banged around in the kitchen, making a large pot of chicken soup she wanted to serve for dinner. I didn't like lying to my father, but Reid was right. Dad wouldn't want to hear I'd spent any time with him, especially since that case had defined the last five years of his law career. No sense in making things worse for him, especially when he was on the road to recovery.

No drama was worth derailing that.

CHAPTER ELEVEN

Reid

“**H**ow long do you think this project is going to take, Mr. Powell?” Walter asked Reid in the kitchen about a week after the record-breaking snowstorm. He picked up a few of the tile samples Reid had ordered online. “From the looks of this, you want to do a complete overhaul of the upstairs bathroom.”

“I do.” Reid moved across the kitchen and poured himself a cup of coffee. “It's starting to look dated.” He turned back to Walter. “Want some?”

“Yes, thank you.” Walter sank into the chair nearest to him, the same kitchen table chair Tarryn sat in only a week before. “I think—”

“What?” Reid poured Walter his cup. He knew the old man liked his coffee with a splash of sugar with no cream, so he didn't ask, he just added it. “You don't like this idea?”

"I don't," Walter said as Reid met him at the kitchen table. "I think you're doing all these repairs for the wrong reason."

"And what reason is that?"

"You're a twenty-nine-year-old man who is hiding."

"Hiding? That how you see it?"

Reid handed Walter his cup, and took a place across from his longtime employee, a man he might have said was also his only friend. No one else had the same history with the Powell family that Walter had, and no one else had dared show him the same loyalty. *It is possibly the only reason I am still civil. Human.*

Walter clasped the warm mug in his wrinkled hands and looked around the kitchen. "I know you've put a lot of work into this old place, and you've done a good job." He chewed over his next words and drank some of his beverage as if the liquid would give him enough strength to make his next point. "But it's like you're blotting out the past with every wall you paint, and every window you change."

Walter was right, of course, but Reid hadn't expected the old man to come right out and say it. Walter usually kept his feelings to himself and wasn't known to question many of Reid's decisions. Those qualities had made the rhythm of their relationship work. If no one pushed back on Reid, he could continue the way he always had, in a comfortable but precarious rhythm. This comment from Walter was... *different.*

"This was our original house, when our family moved here back in the nineteenth century." Reid chose to address Walter's comments directly and drank his coffee. He liked it black, with one small scoop of sugar. "The place was almost falling down when I moved in. Don't you think she deserves a second chance?"

"But what are you going to do with it all when you're done?" Walter frowned. "And will you *ever* be done?"

"One day."

"Then what? You'll keep living out here alone?"

Now it was Reid's turn to frown. "I'm not sure yet." He took a careful sip of coffee. "And why do you care, anyway?"

"Because I care about *you*, Mr. Powell."

"Don't call me that." *I'll never deserve to be called my father's name.* The words came out a little too sharp, and Reid sighed. Once again, he sounded angrier and different than he wanted. "I didn't mean that to sound so abrupt. I'm not... I know you care, Walter." He waved his hand. "I appreciate the concern about what I'm doing here. I just... I'm working through stuff."

"And that means a new guest bathroom."

Reid nodded.

"Okay," Walter said on a sigh. "I suppose I can't convince you otherwise."

The two men finished their drinks and began their task for the day, which was unrelated to the bathroom. They needed to finish painting the third bedroom on the second floor. Reid had decided it needed a new look, too. He didn't like the pale blue, and instead favored light gray. They had one more wall to paint, the largest in the room.

Walter and Reid worked in silence for most of the morning. Their effort had a symbiotic flow that came from two people who knew each other well, and who could read each other. They didn't need to speak.

"We need more paint," Walter said about halfway through the job. "I'll get it."

"It's out in the barn." Reid had a roller in his hand and stood at the top of the A-frame ladder. "Do you remember where it is? On the left-hand side, on the shelves."

Walter put his hands on his hips and regarded the walls. "We're really getting there."

Reid dipped the roller in the paint tray. "It will do, I guess."

"Kind of like this property," Walter replied before he padded out of the room. "It will do."

Reid turned back to the wall, stretching what remained of the paint over the wall. He liked how it was turning out, and a satisfied smile pulled at his lips. It was as if he was a delicate surgeon and this house was his patient. Once he made it better, maybe his life would get better too.

Reid spread another long streak. The paint made a wet, slapping sound as it coated the old plaster. He liked that, it was the noise that came with covering something up, of blotting out what had once been good with something greater. Each stroke was like a stitch. A change. The sad part was, he could cover up the past of the old farmhouse.

He couldn't do the same with his life. *"But what are you going to do with it all when you're done? And will you ever be done?"* Would he ever be done? Would anyone ever live within these walls again? That's what Walter had really been asking. Would there ever be life within this land again? *Because I'm existing. Not living.*

Walter returned after about ten minutes, holding the last can of gray.

"Hey, I was meaning to ask you something. Is this yours?" Walter held up a thin silver chain with a woven pendant. "I found it on the ground near the front steps."

"You did?" Reid regarded the pendant, and he knew exactly who it belonged to. "It's not mine, but I know the owner."

"Really?" Walter let out a satisfied huff. "Then, you're not up here all alone, after all, are you?"

Maybe, maybe not. Reid was sure the lovely Tarryn Long wouldn't be quick to return to his home. He bit down on the inside of his bottom lip. He didn't know how to describe her to his longtime employee.

So he didn't.

Tarryn

One night about a week after the big snowstorm, I got off work early. The night was crisp, and had a charge to it, as if the promise of something new hung in the air. In a way, it did. Dad's speech was slowly improving, and his gross motor movements were becoming more natural, which he was very happy about. Fine motor skills took longer, but he knew this, and so far, had been patient. With him feeling better, I decided as I walked out of the store that I'd head over to One-Way Tavern for an after-work glass of beer. Or maybe some wine. Something.

The place hummed with early evening traffic, and I took in the homey atmosphere as I walked inside. Several patrons already sat at the stools surrounding the bar, a small group played pool in the corner, and every TV in the establishment lit up with twenty-four-hour coverage of college and professional basketball games. I took a seat on the far end of the bar, and ordered my usual Killian's Irish Red.

"You're lucky," Carter said when he returned with it. He hadn't taken my order, but he'd decided to deliver it. He placed the bottle on a cocktail napkin in front of me. "This is on special right now. Happy hour."

"That so? I didn't realize you did a happy hour."

"It's new. We're testing it out, and everything on the drink menu is two-for-one." He smiled at me, and I noticed his handsome features looked less tired than they had a few weeks back. "What do you think? We're looking for customer feedback."

"I approve."

Glancing at the rest of the patrons, I drank some of the full-bodied beer. A few folks had familiar faces from their shopping trips to Country Market, but I didn't know most of them by name. Even with my job and my dad's position in the community, the people of Allen remained a mystery. They held me at bay, as if they didn't want me to get too close.

"Once these folks find out about a deal like this, you'll sell out of bottles," I said.

Carter laughed and leaned across the bar. I caught a whiff of what smelled like peppermint aftershave. "I don't think you understand—this isn't a happy hour for everyone. Just for *you*."

I moved my head away and studied him. *He's flirting with me.* I didn't know how I felt about that. I was confused. No doubt, plenty of people would have called Carter desirable, and even successful. But I'd never felt much for him beyond the benign friendship that came with our childhood. Besides, Carter seemed—*old*. Haggard in some way. Sad.

"You don't have to do me any special favors," I said.

"Why not?" His gaze traced my jawline, then my neck. The light behind his eyes told me he liked what he saw, and that made the hairs on the back of my neck stand to attention. "I know you work hard, and it hasn't exactly been a simple thing to uproot your life and come here to the far side of Ohio." His gaze met mine. "So why can't someone do something nice for you?"

"That's great but—" I started to wave him off, to tell him I wasn't sure I was interested in him like that, when a tumble of men burst through the front door of the bar. They were a bundle of boots, thick coats, and cold. As they moved toward the bar, Carter frowned.

"Mark, why are you here right now?" Carter's frown deepened.

Mark grunted and sat down in one of the open seats. "They let us off early today."

Mark's friends followed his lead and took over some of the other open barstools. None of them looked happy. In fact, stricken was probably a better word.

Carter moved away from me and traveled toward them. Everything about their body language told me something was very wrong. "What happened?"

"They're closing the plant. Shutting it down," one of Mark's companions said as Carter reached them.

"What?" Carter's question was almost a shout. "What do you mean?"

"We're all losing our jobs," Mark added. "The whole plant."

"The whole place?" I asked.

"Two thousand people work at Harper Automotive, and it's all ending in a few weeks."

"Oh my God," I said, and the words came out as a strangled whisper.

All the air seemed to go out of the bar, and the energy changed from a regular relaxed Friday afternoon to that of a supercharged moment. Harper Automotive's main plant operated about twenty minutes away from Allen. Even I knew that most of the region's manufacturing workers found solace at that plant—the ones who remained, at least. While Powell Steel and other companies had closed a long time ago, Harper Automotive had hung on, staying open even through the worst moments of the Great Recession.

It might have been a dinosaur, but at least it was a walking one. And now they were saying it was dead too.

"This is so sad." I got up from my stool and walked over to the group of men. I might not have known them well, but I felt awful about the news, and dread grew in my stomach. "Absolutely horrible."

The men grumbled thanks, and then Carter said, "Whatever you're drinking today, it's on the house. No question about that."

They placed a few orders, but it did little to dull the sharpness in the room. This might be the death blow to Allen, and every one of us felt it. Whatever dignity remained wouldn't stick around town once the region's last major employer shut its doors. The slide had started long ago, but this felt like worse than the bottom.

This felt like a pit of quicksand.

CHAPTER TWELVE

Reid

He drove to Country Market with the necklace in the console cup holder. A few times, he looked at it. Tarryn had good taste, and that showed in the delicate features of the pendant. He wondered if she'd noticed she'd lost it. *She probably has no idea where it is.*

What a stroke of luck to have the chance to give it to her again. He would get to talk to her. *Her.* Get to find out how she was doing. Get to just... know her some more. And yes, he'd been trying to figure out a way to do that ever since she'd climbed into the tow truck on the afternoon after the snowstorm.

He parked in front of the grocery store and considered whether to go inside. He wasn't sure she'd be at work, but he'd assumed there was a fair chance. If she wasn't there, he knew he'd probably find her at her dad's house. Either way, he wanted to return the necklace to her in person.

Reid glanced at the clock. Just after five thirty. The store would stay open a few more hours. He looked through the storefront windows, searching for Marlena. She wouldn't want to see him, so he'd have to weigh his options if she was on the floor.

But he didn't see Marlena.

Can I do this? Should I?

After a few more moments of consideration, he got out of the car, prepared to head inside the store and return the silver necklace. This wouldn't be a big deal if he didn't make it one. But then movement across the street caught his eye.

It was Tarryn, coming out of One-Way Tavern. Tarryn, wearing a dark gray winter coat and a purple hat with a ball of yarn on top. Tarryn, with a frown on her face. Tarryn, accompanied by *Carter Monroe*.

"Shit," Reid muttered.

Maybe he should get back into the truck and leave. Carter didn't like him—no, he *hated* him, something Reid had learned about a year ago, when they ran into each other at a gas station a few townships over from Allen. Carter had confronted him and made it clear that he held a grudge. And Reid didn't feel like discussing the past right then.

But—

"*Reid?*" Tarryn called from across the lot. "Is that you?"

Too late.

"Yeah." Reid shut the door and trudged across to them. Tarryn looked happy to see him, but Carter had narrowed eyes and a scrunched face. He nodded at him, hoping that if he was friendly, Carter might be, too. "How are you, Carter? Tarryn?"

"Okay. We're… yeah… we're okay." Tarryn glanced at Carter. "Carter was walking me to my car… and um—"

"She means that we've been better," Carter said. "Not that you give a damn about anyone but yourself."

Reid held the necklace in his left hand, and he gripped it tighter. He decided to ignore Carter and focus on Tarryn. "What about your car? Is it fixed?"

"It's in the shop and will probably take about two more weeks to fix. Thanks for helping me." She nodded across the lot. "At this point, I'm driving Dad's old Lincoln. He's not using it, anyway." She frowned. "So"—she and Carter exchanged looks— "I guess—"

"Is something wrong?" Reid asked.

Tarryn shoved her gloved hands in the pockets of her coat and hunched her shoulders. "Harper Automotive is closing. They just broke the news this afternoon, and a couple of the guys came into the bar for beer."

"What?"

Shock rolled over Reid as he forced out the question. This *was* bad news, horrible news. The kind of blow that everyone in the valley would feel, whether they worked at the plant or not. This was a death rattle for Allen. Reid heard it, loud and clear.

"When?"

"End of next month." Carter grimaced. "They're moving the operations to Mexico, or some other fucking place."

Reid's heart beat a little faster. Harper Automotive had stepped in where his family had failed, offering a lifeline to the region once the Powells ceded their spot as the largest employer. Harper might have only been a third the size of the old steel company, but its infusion of jobs had kept plenty of families in Allen from sinking.

But not now. Not anymore.

"I'm... god, I'm sorry." Reid knew the words didn't sound sincere, and didn't offer much solace, but he said them anyway. *This isn't news anyone wants to hear.*

"Yeah, whatever." Carter shook his head as he crossed his arms and turned to Tarryn. "I should get back into the bar. Are you okay here, or—"

"I'm fine." She gave him a smile, and Reid found himself studying every moment of it. Did she like Carter? Was there a *thing* between them?

"Goodnight."

"Goodnight, Tarryn."

Carter let out another sigh and made his way to the employee parking lot off to the side of the bar. Reid felt relief make its way from his neck to his back, and he refused to regret it. This was what he came for—he was going to get his chance to talk to Tarryn after all.

"That closure is awful news," Reid said once they were alone.

"Horrible. Like a bomb went off, and even that's a meaningless way to put it. Where are these people going to work? They don't have many options."

"No, they don't."

"They were so upset when they came into the bar." A hollow expression crossed Tarryn's face. "They were dazed, in a way. Like they'd been punched."

Reid swallowed. He knew that look; he loathed it. Reid first saw it the day his father announced the closure of Powell Steel. He was twelve at the time and stood next to his dad, mom, and Logan on a hastily erected dais in the middle of the factory floor. A low rumble coursed through the crowd when his father broke the news. Some people cried out. A few wept. One man yelled, "You promised you'd keep this open."

And it seemed like a raincloud had gathered above them all, dropping a torrential downpour on the whole community, a monsoon that never stopped.

Reid shuddered at the memory. "When a person doesn't have a job, doesn't have a purpose, it does something to them." His shoulders slumped. "This is my fault."

Tarryn recoiled. "You didn't have anything to do with this."

"But Allen is what it is—because of my family, Tarryn. We made a fortune off this town, and the labor that came with it. Everyone depended on our company to keep the gears going. And we didn't. We failed."

To his surprise, she shook her head. "That's ridiculous. You didn't force Harper Automotive to close."

"I know, but it's the same as when my father—"

"Stop. I might not know the whole history of everything that's happened in this town, but from what I've learned in life so far, one person isn't to blame for absolutely everything that goes wrong."

"I don't think you get it. Those men—"

"Those men—those people—have to go home to their families and tell them they won't be able to provide for them anymore. They're frustrated. They feel hopeless.

And it's bullshit." He heard the anger in her voice, and Reid had to admit he liked seeing the fire in her. She was so *protective* of this place, even though she'd spent less time here than anyone else he knew. "You know what, Reid? You're never going to get anywhere if you keep pitying yourself."

"Excuse me?"

She pulled her coat closer to her body to ward off the creeping cold before taking a step closer to him. "Keep sulking like that, and your life is going to become a self-fulfilling prophesy."

His eyes widened. No one had spoken that bluntly to him in a long time, not even Walter. Reid struggled to think of a reply. How did he explain himself to her? "You've... ah... you've seen the way people treat me."

"Because you let them." She looked him squarely in the eye, holding his gaze for a breath. "Because that's the narrative you want to put out there."

"Come on, I—"

"Stop." She jerked her head in the direction of the bar. "I know you think all the people in there, and everyone else in town hate you. And maybe they do. But they also haven't had the chance to see anything else about you. They don't see your other side. Like the one you showed me the other week, during the snowstorm. No one sees that, do they?"

"No."

She clicked her teeth. "Maybe if you let them, they'd treat you differently."

With those words, Tarryn nodded once, said goodbye to Reid, walked over to her car, and drove away.

Reid watched her go and stared at the empty space where her vehicle had been for a long time. After a while, he looked at the necklace in his hand, which he'd clutched hard enough during their conversation to make an indentation in his palm. He tucked the necklace into his coat pocket. Tarryn's final words echoed in his head. Maybe if he *did* let the rest of the townspeople see him, they *would* treat him differently.

He wasn't sure he wanted to take that risk.

CHAPTER THIRTEEN

Tarryn

I was out of breath when I got home, and my heart beat as fast as if I'd gone for a six-mile run. I pulled the car into the driveway and sat in it for a few minutes with the engine running. I willed myself to settle down, but it didn't work. And I didn't know what had keyed me up more—the news about Harper Automotive or seeing Reid again.

Reid. Reid Powell.

He was handsome, in a broken, troubled way. I'd been thinking that as I laid down my challenge outside the bar. Reid Powell had a deep, kind, heartfelt side to him, and I'd seen a few glimpses of it during my overnight stay. If he kept that side of himself hidden away from everyone forever, it would be a shame. It would be a huge loss. For everyone.

Still thinking about it, I pulled my phone out of my purse and opened the internet browser app. I typed "Powell" "Accident" and "Allen" into the search bar and took a deep breath.

Over eighty thousand hits returned in the browser results.

That shouldn't have surprised me, but it did. I scrolled through the first few pages of hits, digesting all kinds of blog posts, articles, and video. It gave me a better idea of how extensive the media had covered both the bus accident and the shutting down of Powell Steel. Each one had received a similar amount of coverage as the other, and I realized for the first-time what weight the past must be on Reid's shoulders. As a teenager, it had been so easy to ignore it all from several hundred miles away in Cincinnati. It didn't disrupt my immediate routine, so what had I cared? Now, up close, I saw all the pockmarks and warts. It would be hard for a lot of communities to come back from *one* of these events, much less two. And now, three?

Still, there had to be another chapter for Reid. For Allen. For all of them. *The past doesn't have to be the future. Right?*

I closed the Internet app and opened my contact list. When I found Amelia's number, I punched call on the screen. She usually preferred text messages, so I was shocked when she picked up. But I was glad. I needed my friend.

"How's it going in Nowhere Ohio?" she asked after we exchanged a quick greeting.

"Not as good as I hoped. But not bad, either. Dad is slowly getting stronger every day. But Allen is... different. It's worse here than I thought it was."

"How so?"

"Just not a lot of hope. Maybe that's the best way to put it." I considered how to frame my next words. "And now, Harper Automotive is closing at the end of the month."

Amelia sucked in a gasp. "Really?"

"Yep. And those are the last decent jobs people have around here."

"But isn't Harper a major company? They own... have all those different businesses, don't they? I always see their ads on TV."

"From what I heard they're getting out of the business of making car parts. Or maybe it's just that they're moving the plant overseas. I don't know, because there are a lot of rumors floating around. But whatever it is, it's a shakeup."

My best friend didn't reply for a few moments. Amelia had also voiced her reservations about me moving to Allen to take care of Dad instead of finishing college, but she'd also always been good at giving me practical advice. And fifteen years of close friendship had given us an unspoken familiarity that couldn't be easily replicated.

"What does your dad think?" she asked.

I sighed. "He's going to be so upset when he hears about it. He takes everything that happens here, every setback, so personally. That's what I think caused the stroke in the first place. He internalized everything, and it just got worse over time."

"Especially since the accident."

I shuddered at the memories, as well as what I'd just seen in the internet search. It wasn't that the accident was the largest in the state, or that the video was sensational. The country had seen far worse. But still, what happened that day had captured the attention of the nation because so many things collided in the story: a family with a waning fortune, a community in the rustiest part of the Rust Belt, several dead children on their way home from school, the opioid epidemic, a handsome man who had fallen on hard times, and his even better-looking older brother.

The media couldn't have scripted it better. They ate up the pain with a greedy vengeance, gnawing on every broken detail. Every chance they could, they revisited it.

"So," I said carefully to Amelia, "the other thing that happened is… I met Reid Powell the other day. The brother of the guy who caused the accident."

"He *still* lives there?"

"Yep." I thought back to the answer Reid have given me about that, about how he considered Allen home no matter how sad things got. "I think he tried to leave once, but this place called him back."

"He must be a masochist." Amelia laughed once at her weak joke. "I mean, his brother killed those kids, right? Why stick around after that?" She smacked her lips together a few times, and I guessed the wheels had begun turning in her head. "What's he like?"

I cleared my throat. I knew her so well that I could have predicted that Amelia would ask that question next. "He's… interesting."

"Oh, come on," She scoffed. "Interesting? That's one of the most meaningless words in the dictionary. Try again."

"What? That word isn't so bad," I replied with mock innocence. "I mean, he is that, he *is* interesting. He's also complicated, to say the least, and way older than I am. But he's nice too."

"Nice. Another empty word."

"Hey, I'm not a wordsmith like you."

She laughed. "So, how did you meet him?"

"He chose to come out of his lair." I grinned at the memory of our night together during the snowstorm. "And I found him."

We finished our chat and said goodbye. I left the car and entered the house. It was still early evening, and Dad sat alone in the living room, watching a rerun of Jeopardy. He lit up as I walked in the room, and I knew he didn't have any clue about what had happened at Harper.

"We need to talk," I said as I sank into the sofa. "It's important, Dad." I regarded him for a beat. "I was down at The One-Way earlier, and a couple of workers came in from Harper Automotive." I gulped. "It's closing in a couple of weeks."

"C-closing?"

"The plant. The whole thing. They're moving to Mexico, I think."

Dad's fork clattered onto the tray in front of him. A sliver of relief traveled across my chest. At least he knew. My dad truly loved this county and the people in it. In a way, I was glad I got to tell him the news, because I had worried what stress it might cause him if he found out via the gossip mill or on the news. I didn't know enough about strokes to understand the relationship between stress and recovery, but I believed caution was the best approach.

"This is devastating," he managed.

"They broke the news this afternoon at a company-wide meeting."

I leaned back on the cushions. My legs were tired, and my shoulders heavy. And I knew if I felt this way, the rest of the town must too. "Dad, I feel so bad about everything. I can't imagine what you must feel about this. I know you've lived and breathed Allen for so many years."

"This... town... is... is falling apart."

"We have to stay optimistic. Even though it's hard." I stood from the couch and headed to the kitchen. In the fridge, I found two Budweiser beers and threw a straw in one. When I returned to the living room with them, I handed one to my dad. "I know it's against doctor's orders, but news like this deserves one."

He gulped down a large swig of the drink. "We need... miracle. A... a hero."

Dad was right. But what could rescue a place that had lost all hope?

CHAPTER FOURTEEN

Reid

He drove home with the Harper Automotive news on his mind. It dominated his thoughts as he made dinner. Wrapped around every breath he took. The people of Allen deserved better than they were getting, better than the hand life had dealt all of them. That night, he didn't sleep.

"What's on your mind?" Walter asked when he came to the back door the following morning. "You're under a bigger cloud than usual."

"Did you hear the news about Harper Auto?"

"No."

Reid motioned for Walter to come inside the house. Walter tapped the snow residue off his work boots and stepped through the doorway. Reid shut the door behind him. "The plant is closing."

Just like everyone else, Walter had wide eyes and a half-open mouth as soon as Reid broke the news. "Oh God. This is *it*, isn't it?"

"All those people out of work." Reid snapped his fingers, which had become dry and cracked from the frigid temperatures. "Just like that."

Walter replied with a slow nod. "Everyone that's left, which isn't many people, considering this county has about a third the population it had twenty-five years ago."

Reid didn't reply. He didn't have to—they both knew what things had been like in Allen a quarter century before. Powell Steel had been the center of it all, a glistening gem of American innovation and manufacturing. How long ago that seemed. How distant.

The two men stared at each other for a long time, and then Walter cleared his throat. The sound pierced the silence that had settled in around them.

"You have to do something, Mr. Powell."

"How many times do I have to tell you to call me Reid? Mr. Powell was my father, and I'm not him."

"Okay, fine. You gotta do something, Reid. It's time." Walter put a cautious hand on his arm. "I know you can."

Reid glanced down at the hand, then jerked his arm from Walter's grasp. "No… no, I don't think so."

"Why not?"

Shaking his head, Reid walked away from his employee then sat at the kitchen table. He sensed where this was going, and he didn't want to take it there.

"This mess is not something I'm sure I can fix." Reid crossed his arms and focused on the snowy hill outside the kitchen window. Deer tracks littered a small path that disappeared into a grove of evergreens. Nearby lay the small cemetery buried with generations of his family. His father had a place there. So did his mother, and Logan. *Logan...* "The problem is too complicated, and besides, they'll *never* look at me as a savior."

"What if they were wrong?"

"But are they?"

Walter let out a long sigh. "Reid, I think you've let yourself become the man they created, not the man you are. You're not a villain who should die a lonely death." His tone turned a little stronger, and Reid was taken aback. His longtime companion and employee almost never spoke to him like this. "What are you doing with that expensive education of yours, anyway?" Walter shook his head. "All of those years at Northwestern and business school for your MBA at what—the University of Chicago, right?"

"No, it was undergrad at Chicago, and then my MBA at Northwestern."

Walter bit back a smile. "Excuse me, then."

"Just saying that for the record."

"But like I suspected, you're prouder of it that you think."

"That was... that was all before the accident," Reid replied. "Before Logan, before I had to come back here to help him, before..." Those degrees felt far away, like pieces of paper he'd obtained in expectation of a life that was never supposed to turn out the way it had.

"Maybe it's not my place to talk about your family's money, but it's time I spoke up," Walter whispered. "You can bring about change. It can come from you. Powell

Steel might have closed, but your family still had a substantial estate. It's how you kept me on all these years."

"It's dirty money."

"So what? Why can't it be used for good rather than stay locked up in some bank account?" Walter pointed his thumb at the window closest to the kitchen table. "Staying here, hiding here... you're worth more than that. Don't allow small-minded people to determine your future. Allen's future. This—here—is a purgatory of your own making."

"What would you have me do? They wanted to incarcerate me for what happened, and they almost did. They blame me for Logan 's mistakes." *They call me trash. Monster.*

"Then make them see what I do. Make them see you a different way." Walter stood from the table. "I think this is worse than any jail anyway. You have so much to give, Reid. You're alive. Go live."

Walter took another long look at Reid, drank the last of his coffee, zipped his jacket a bit tighter, and headed to the garage to set up for more painting. Reid stared after him a long time, and Walter's last words echoed in his mind. *You're alive. Go live.*

Reid got up from the kitchen table and stomped upstairs to the third floor. The attic spanned the upstairs perimeter of the farmhouse, at the top of a steep staircase covered in threadbare carpet. The space featured a hodgepodge of boxes, some dusty furniture covered by sheets, and a whole lot of memories. Some of them welcome, a lot of them not.

Reid headed to the far corner of the attic. He yanked a dusty sheet off a large trunk that he'd packed up years ago, and sworn he'd never look at again. Just like a lot of things he wanted to forget, he'd managed to keep its contents locked away.

But Walter's words had triggered something inside him. *You can bring about change. It can come from you.* Could he turn this town around? Dare he even think that way?

He took a deep breath and opened the trunk. Stale cedar escaped into the air, filling his nostrils with a mix of heavy wood and preservation. Inside the trunk were two smaller boxes, a few binders, and three sets of photo albums.

He chose the first album and opened the leather cover. The pages stuck together, and he flipped through them carefully, looking at pictures he remembered and many he'd forgotten. Black and whites of his parents on their wedding day. Grainy polaroid snaps of family vacations to Florida and North Carolina. A few yellowed images of his time at a summer camp in northern Michigan.

But most of the photos in this album were of Logan. Logan as a baby. As a toddler in a snowsuit and small clown outfit for Halloween. Logan in a navy jacket outside holding hands with their mother as they walked to church on Sunday. Logan with feathered hair and thick glasses. Logan as a teenager in a green Nirvana T-shirt in his seventh-grade photo.

Logan before their mother's death.

Logan before their father's death.

Logan before heroin.

Reid slammed the album shut. Too painful to look at them anymore, even though he'd known that would be the case. Life back then was simpler, and easier, and he needed those memories. They fueled the other things in the trunk.

He put the album aside and grabbed a metal box from the back of the trunk, along with a few binders of aging paper. He hadn't looked at either for years, but that didn't matter. He'd memorized the words inside the box a long time ago. Still, he wanted to see them again.

With a tentative hand, he opened the box. He shifted through the letters and documents he saved from when his mother and father died. The crumbling rubber band holding them together broke apart. A rueful laugh escaped his lips. He was a hoarder and he knew it. A hoarder of the past. And of his pain.

His father's last letter was on top of the pile. He wrote it before the brain cancer took away his memories, before becoming a victim to his disease. Reid remembered how his father's attorney delivered it after the funeral, after reading the will that explained what remained of the Powell assets. The distinctive script of the letter was faded but legible. It had three paragraphs, and the last one stood out the most.

You've always been the responsible, levelheaded one. I know you can restore dignity to our family and to Allen. You can succeed where I failed. You must try. Promise me that you will, and that you won't give up. That you will follow through with the talents and gifts you have. Take care of Logan. Take care of yourself. And take care of this place.

He took out the top binder and blew away the dust that coated it. Beneath the green cover lay a myriad of printed spreadsheets, documents, drawings, a proposed budget, account balance statements, and projections. He thumbed through the pages, remembering how much effort he'd put into the work six years earlier, when he'd spent the fall outlining how he wanted to restore the Powell family to greatness in the valley around Allen. He'd been flush with cash, and bursting with ideas about Powell Advanced Robotics, the company he wanted to create with Logan at his side.

He'd had *hope*.

All the work Reid had done in business school seemed destined to culminate in this project, this one moment of glory that he'd believed would eventually bring a few thousand jobs to the area and a new breath of life to the region.

Then the wreck happened. And he'd boxed up his plans. It had felt right to do so back then, to shut away whatever dreams he'd wanted for a different life. He'd never live up to his father's words. Reid had failed him, and failed Logan too.

Except, maybe it was time for a change. *You're worth more than that. Don't let small-minded and unforgiving people determine your future. Allen's future.* God, he wanted Walter to be right.

More than that, Reid *needed* it.

CHAPTER FIFTEEN

Tarryn

The news coated everything in the town with a dull film of despair. It wasn't visible to the naked eye, but I saw it in the slumped shoulders of the people who came into Country Market, heard it in their grumbling voices, and felt it in their wary gazes. Things were bad. Really bad.

"Would you like paper or plastic?" I asked Mrs. Needleman, as I began to check her out on an evening a few nights after my encounter with Reid outside The One-Way Tavern. She came into the store twice a week and told me once that her husband worked as a foreman at Harper Automotive. She'd backed that up with a shiny debit card from the company's credit union.

"Paper," she mumbled as she took a wallet from her weather-beaten leather purse. She yanked a few ragged coupons out of it and handed them over to me. "You take these, right?"

"We do." I took them from her hand and began organizing the pile. "I heard the news," I murmured. "About Harper."

"Yeah, well, have you heard what they're offering out there?"

Her tone of voice sent a pulse of dread through me. I shook my head.

"Practically nothing." She sneered. "One-month severance and a few other fringe benefits. That's it. After all this time, that's all Michael's getting." She glanced out of the large picture windows of the store, as if she thought she'd find an answer behind them. "Fifteen years of his life. For *that*."

My heart sank. She often bought chicken fingers, sugary snacks, and fruit juice, so I knew she had kids at home. *What will they do now? How will they take care of their families?*

No good answers for those questions.

I looked over my shoulder in search of Marlena. A few moments before, she'd been in aisle seven, restocking the store selection of cereal. I didn't see her there now and couldn't locate her in any other part of the sales floor.

"I'm so sorry," I said as I turned back to Mrs. Needleman.

"Sorry isn't enough these days. *Everyone* is sorry."

I regarded the small pile of groceries Mrs. Needleman planned to buy. A quick addition in my head told me the whole thing would cost less than forty-five dollars. I had that on me. I didn't have much, but I had that. In fact, Nora gave me cash that morning to grab a few items from the pharmacy for Dad. I could easily use my credit card instead. "You know what?" I met her gaze. "Don't worry about any of this right now. It's taken care of."

Her eyes bulged. "What?"

"You heard me." I waved a hand, hoping she'd feel at ease, and wouldn't question the gift too much. "Special secret sale for our best customers. And you happen to be one of our best ones."

She cocked her head. "Are you sure? I can pay, and—"

"I'm sure." I picked up a packet of hot dogs and put it in one of the paper bags at the end of the register. "Like I said, this is a deal for one of our most loyal customers."

She studied me for a beat, as if expecting me to tell her it was all a joke. I didn't.

"Thank you." Her shoulders visibly relaxed and a few of the wrinkles in her face softened. "You don't... you don't have any clue what this means."

I probably didn't, but I could guess.

I smiled at her. "Everyone needs a break, right? Even you."

"Thanks." She picked up a packet of cheese and put it in a second bag. "Wow, I've never received something like that from here before. You're really nice to do this."

"Don't mention it."

We packed up the rest of her purchases, and when she left the store, I fished fifty dollars out of my pocket and slid it in the cash register. What Marlena didn't know wouldn't hurt her. And besides, it felt good to do that for someone else.

112

But something else nagged at me as soon as I paid for the groceries.

What was going to happen to the rest of this town?

After my shift, I walked over to One-Way Tavern for another after-work drink. I figured I might hear more of the gossip in town if I did, and besides, it was the only place in Allen to really unwind after a long day. I ordered my typical beer and took a seat at the far end of the bar. A handful of patrons fanned out from there playing pool and darts, but the establishment was mostly empty.

"Long day?" Carter asked as he walked over to me, carrying a cloth towel. He wiped his hands on it a few times and put it down on the shelf closest to a line of well liquors. "You look tired."

"I am. Today was stock day at the store, so we had a lot of cataloging to do."

"Lot of people come in?"

"A few." I drank some beer and felt his eyes roam over me. I'd seen that look before from him, and I hoped he wouldn't try to act on it. "But the biggest thing was unpacking the stock."

He moved closer to the bar and braced one arm on it. "I wonder how the news about the plant is going to affect the sales at Country Market."

"I don't really know. I guess it depends on what work comes up for those now unemployed." I decided not to add that I had already seen that happen. "But we'll get through it, won't we? This town can bounce back from this, can't they?"

His face fell. "I'm not too sure about that, Tarryn. Without any real investment, we might not be able to get through this one."

I wondered if any conversations from here forward would ever not circle back to this issue, this noose around the neck of the people in my father's beloved community. "We need something. A way out of this. Anything."

"Did you hear about the community meeting next week? On Monday?"

I shook my head.

"It's at the Allen Community Center. At seven." He held up an index finger to signal me to wait, then he walked down the length of the bar. Carter returned with a flyer in his hand, showing it to me.

"Wow." I took the paper from him and read the details. The mayor's office wanted a public hearing, and the notice asked anyone interested to attend.

"They just set up the meeting last night. I think it's to discuss what we can do next, if anything."

"I see that." I gave the paper back to him. "I wonder if Mayor Johnson has a plan."

Carter scoffed. "That guy is a total waste. He's more focused on furthering himself than he is in the people of this community. He's never had a decent idea in his life."

I laughed without humor. "That's harsh, don't you think?"

Carter spread a calloused hand. "I mean, have you seen Allen lately?"

"I have."

"Then I rest my case."

I downed another gulp of beer. The drink had warmed, and the liquid tickled my throat. "I get what you're saying, Carter. You have a right to be critical of people you think aren't doing enough."

"You know, I tried with this bar." Carter's voice turned heavy. "Did the best I could. I wanted to invest in this place because no one else would. But now I feel like I don't know what else to do. And then I think about Laura—" He tightened his fist. "Let's just say I have my own opinions about who really started all the downslide around here. And some people haven't been held accountable for their share of the responsibility."

His expression had hardened, and a darkness seemed to fall over him. I gaped at him, unable to come up with a decent reply. Carter Monroe was a lot angrier than I previously realized.

But maybe that's justified.

"Well, umm… we… surely we'll get some answers at the meeting next week," I choked out, and hoped my words sounded more optimistic than I felt. "There has to be some way forward for everyone."

"I sure hope so." Carter nodded at the beer bottle. "Can I get you another one of those?"

"No, thank you." I pushed the empty bottle and cocktail napkin away from me. "I should keep it to just one, since I'm driving."

He smiled, and the expression on his face turned marginally kinder. "You know, all sadness about this town aside, I'm really glad you came in here." He moved closer to me again and lowered his voice. "I've been meaning to ask you something."

I sucked in a deep breath. A sense of foreboding wrapped around me, and I guessed what it was before he even asked it.

"Want to have dinner with me on Saturday?" Carter asked. "I know a great little Italian place in Youngstown, near the square. We can go there." He let out a nervous laugh. "Maybe escape this town for a while. Get some fresh air."

I studied him for a moment. This was a date. Definitely. No question about that. He wasn't asking me out as a friend or to do a good deed. Carter wanted more from me.

But how can I turn down someone who is so wounded? I can't hurt him even more, can I?

"Okay," I said, fighting back the doubts in my stomach. "I can't do Saturday because I need to stay home and help Dad around the house. But, how about Friday? Will that work?"

He grinned. "Friday is perfect. Turns out that being the owner of this place does have at least one benefit. I get to pick my nights off."

I smiled back. Spending time with Carter wouldn't be too bad. This was only dinner.

Right?

CHAPTER SIXTEEN

Tarryn

The morning after I accepted Carter's invitation to dinner, I woke up with my mind racing. I hadn't slept more than a few restless hours, and I had a crick in my neck.

I threw on my workout clothes, grabbed my wallet, tucked my phone in my pocket, and stretched my aching neck. It popped a few times, and I winced. *I really do need a break. The stress of what is going on here is getting to me.* When I walked into the kitchen, Nora and my dad were seated at the table. She had a cup of coffee between her hands, and there was a newspaper between them. They both greeted me with a smile, but then Nora's face fell.

"You look like you barely slept. Are you okay, Tarryn?"

"Yeah, I am." I sat in one of the empty chairs. "Just have a lot on my mind. I don't know... I just... I'm worried."

"Everyone is." Nora sipped her drink. "My stepbrother is one of those losing a job at Harper. Has two kids under five. He says his best option is to go to Cleveland and try to find work there."

"More expensive... to live," my dad said, and I took a moment to think about that.

"Yeah, and that's a problem, Dad. Living in any of those big cities is much more expensive than living in Allen. What a horrible situation, Nora."

"It hasn't been a good couple of days."

I was sure that was an understatement of the century, but I did appreciate Nora's ability to soften the blow a little. No doubt Dad did too. She brought a lot of calm to both of us.

"I hope he can get a new job," I said.

"I hope he can too." Nora turned her attention to the newspaper. Conversation over, for now.

A few minutes later, I stood from the table. "I'm going for a run. I'll be back soon."

I managed one mile before I realized how disconnected my legs were from my head. I hated runs like that. They were always so much of a struggle, and almost not worth the effort. Annoyed, I ducked into Karl's Kitchen, a small grab-and-go diner that was the only place open in Allen that early in the morning. It was almost vacant, and the waitress seemed surprised to see me. I took a spot at the dingy counter, ordered an orange juice, and once again opened the Internet browser on my phone.

My thumbs flew across the keypad as I typed in a search once more about the Powell family. Something I'd seen in the results before my conversation with Amelia had stayed with me, like a signal flag. I wasn't sure I'd be able to find it again, but as I sipped the juice, a few things came into better focus. Once, the affluence of the Powell family and Allen had resembled each other. Martin Powell moved west to make his fortune in the 1870s, took advantage of the industrial era, and brought steel to Allen in 1882. He grew Powell Steel into one of the biggest mills west of Pittsburgh, and by 1915, the company employed more than four thousand people. At that time, Allen was a thriving small town with a movie theater, department store, four hotels, and a white tableclothed restaurant on Main Street. On the weekends, everyone from the surrounding townships and counties came to Allen to pass the time at one of the many festivals and revivals that dotted the community every year.

And while the rest of the Rust Belt might have suffered from economic decline starting in the late 1970s, Powell Steel managed to stay steady, an example of American manufacturing and innovation, a company whose CEO vowed he'd keep it all going no matter what.

Until a few years after 9/11, when Powell Steel suddenly closed. Soon after, the hotels were gone, too, along with the fancy restaurant and the downtown movie theater. Newton Department Store closed in 2010, at the end of the Great Recession.

Then came the accident.

But none of this was what I wanted. I opened the images section on the browser and scrolled through the results there too. And then I found it on the fourth page. There was Reid Powell, in a graduation cap and gown, proudly holding his MBA degree from the Kellogg School of Management at Northwestern.

I clicked on the image. I read about his master's in business and found his thesis posted online. Most of the details were way over my head, but one thing did stand out from the index— *"Why robotics isn't synonymous with layoffs. How to build and keep a workforce."*

And when I was done reading it all, I sat back in my chair, more than a little stunned. *What if he can be the answer? What it all comes down to him?* Reid Powell was a very intelligent man. What if there was more than just a thesis? Had he given this any thought since finishing his degree?

I got up from the counter stool and gestured at the waitress, who stood in front of the register near the far end. "Thanks for the drink," I said as I placed a five-dollar bill on the counter. I was out the door seconds later, and this time my feet didn't feel so disconnected from my head.

They carried me all the way to Springhill Lane. With each step, my thoughts kept going back to Reid, and the pain I saw behind his eyes. I wanted to talk to him. Needed to. It couldn't wait.

Plus, he hadn't placed any orders at the store, or shopped at Country Market any of the times I'd been working over the last two weeks.

So, I was concerned, in a way.

More like curious, Tarryn.

A few moments after eight, I arrived at the entrance to his road. The morning was still, the air crisp, and the cold still threatening. I wasn't sure I had the right to approach Reid about this issue, but *nothing ventured, nothing gained.* Throughout the run, I argued back and forth inside my head, but by the time I was only a few feet away, I was resolved. *It was time Reid gave something back.*

Reid's snow-covered truck was in the driveway on the property, so I knew he was home. When I got to the porch, I bounded up the steps and rang the doorbell.

No backing down now.

He answered the door a few seconds after I rang it, and I wondered if he was almost waiting for me to arrive. He wore a flannel shirt with jeans, and he carried a coffee mug.

"You're awake," I said, not bothering to say hello.

"I like to get up early." He leaned against the door frame, and I noticed that he'd shaved. He also looked well-rested and less haggard than the last time I'd seen him. *God, that jawline...* "Can I help you with something? Maybe get you a cup of coffee?"

"No, I'm fine, I just had some orange juice."

"Good."

He stared at me, and a flush of embarrassment pulsed from my knees to my throat. Here I stood, an uninvited guest, trespassing on his property, once again showing up unannounced, kicking down an invisible wall that seemed wrapped around him. *What the heck am I thinking?*

"I'm sorry," I blurted. "Sometimes, I have trouble with boundaries. I get something in my mind, and—"

"Don't worry about it. I'll let it slide." He tossed me a wry smile that somehow seemed warmer than any he'd given me so far, then glanced inside his house. "Do you want to come in?"

"Yes. I think I will." A sigh of relief escaped my chest before I wiped my shoes on the doormat and followed his lead.

"So, what brings you out here?" He shut the door behind us. "I don't think I have any outstanding orders at Country Market."

"You don't." A nervous laugh escaped my lips. "I don't have that excuse." I took a seat on the small bench in the foyer. It felt good to sit down, and the muscles in my legs twitched from the exercise. "But I've been thinking about you a lot lately."

"Really? Should I be pleased?"

"Maybe, but not necessarily in that way." *Gah.* The man flustered me. If it was because he was so good-looking, I wasn't sure, but I was here on a mission, and I shouldn't let his mild flirtation distract me. *Is he flirting? He really shouldn't smile around me...* "Just... have you heard about what they're offering people for severance down at the plant? At Harper?"

"I have." Still gripping his coffee cup, Reid sat on the bench across from me. "Walter mentioned it a few days ago."

"It's terrible. Awful. I don't know how else to describe it. Like a bomb went off, but no one is coming to clean up the mess."

Those were the kinds of statements I heard from bewildered people on the news, like the people who were interviewed when a school shooting or a hurricane occurred in their town. They were meaningless at best, and a helpless description of what was really going on in the area. My stomach lurched. *This must work.*

"And after that, what are all those people going to do for jobs?" I asked. "Where are they going to turn next?"

He raised a hand as if he wanted me to calm down. "Allen will survive. It always does."

I shuddered. "You sound so... so clinical about this. As if you've just accepted it."

"I haven't *accepted* anything. I know who the people are in this part of the country. They don't roll over and die, no matter what. They figure things out."

I gulped. This wasn't going the way I hoped at all, the way I had envisioned on my run. Time to try another tactic. The Powells had been a proud family, and Reid, despite his reluctance, had that same blood running through his veins. But I couldn't be the one to throw the idea at him, to use his brains and his degree. No, it had to come from him. Which meant I had to play a role here to ensure he believed he could make a difference. *I* believed in him, but at the end of the day, he had to believe in himself first.

Can I get him there?

"I don't understand why you keep yourself shut away. Why you won't lift a finger to help this region you say you love." I made a wild gesture at the front door and all that lay outside it. "Your family was once the most important one in this whole town. The most important one for fifty miles. And it's like you... it's like you *abdicated* your responsibility."

"Abdicated? I'm not royalty."

I thought about what I'd read on my phone a short time before. "You were once. Your family ruled this town, and when they were at their best, so was Allen."

Reid pursed his lips. The seam made a flat line that pinched his face. "That's an overstatement, and it's more complicated than that, Tarryn."

"Is it? It seems a whole lot simpler than you're making it." I'd sunk my teeth into the issue, and my stubbornness wouldn't let me release the hold until I got what I wanted. "For God's sake, you're still young. I know you're smart and resourceful. These people need you, and you could really make a difference here. In this town."

He cocked his head. "How do you suggest that I do that?"

"By doing something." I was growing frustrated, and it coated my voice. I hadn't thought through all my ideas, so I was swinging at anything. Anything to get him there. "Don't you have millions tucked away somewhere? That's what people think around here. They think you have a fortune, that your family ended up with millions even after Powell Steel closed, and you won't use any of it to help anyone else."

"And they think I got all that money off the backs of their relatives," he added. "I'm aware of what they think. It's blood money."

"What if you invested it in Allen? Invested it in yourself?" I sighed and raised both my hands. "Not my business at all. But I think—"

"How much money do you think I have, Tarryn?"

"Enough. Enough to help. There are plenty of people here with skills that the world could use. But what if you can help them stay here? If people don't want to leave Allen, couldn't you bring the work to Allen?" I glanced around the farmhouse foyer. "Besides, doesn't it get lonely out here in your self-imposed exile?"

"Sometimes. A lot of times."

"So why not come out into the land of the living?"

Reid shook his head. "Trust me, it won't work. Forgiveness isn't something the people around here want to give."

I pressed my back against the wall. He'd given up on himself, hadn't he? On his family. On his town.

"You have to show them that you want it," I finally replied. "You have to show them you've come to terms with what happened, and the ugliness of the past. It's only fair. They were hurt. They went through a lot."

"So did my family." His face fell. "I lost the last piece of family that I had that day. The last person who knew me for *me*, and not because I was a Powell, or because my relatives had once been a big deal around here."

"If you want someone to know the real you, you have to let them in. You have to let them see you." My shoulders heaved.

"What have you heard about my brother?"

I decided to temper my reply. "Not a lot. Just that he caused the accident."

He frowned. "That's a shame. Logan was a good person, despite what people say. The heroin and the painkillers took away the part of him I loved. For the longest time, I thought I could fix him. I thought if I offered him enough support, and gave him enough chances, he'd be able to get through the weeds and go back to the way he used to be. But the drugs were like a snake wrapped around him."

I heard something in his voice, a sharpness that hadn't been there before, a bitterness that came out the strongest when Reid got to the part about how much the drugs had taken over his brother's life.

No one ever asks him about Logan, do they?

"Tell me about him," I tried, realizing how lonely it must be for him to be the only person to still remember the good in someone after they had died. "Not about the drugs. About your brother. What's your best memory of him?"

Reid frowned. "Are you sure you want to know?"

"If I didn't, I wouldn't have asked."

"Fair enough." Reid took a deep breath. "People don't like to talk about who he was before. They want to focus on what happened, as if that accident defined him— defined us."

"People are cruel, especially now." I took my phone out of my jacket pocket and wagged it at him. "And these stupid things only make that worse. People use it as a shield, and they write things on social media they would never say to someone in person."

"Thank God that accident happened before the Internet is what it is now." He sighed. "It would have only been a thousand times more horrific."

I decided to not say anything. I let him speak and made sure to remain focused on him. I wanted Reid to know I was listening—I was *hearing* him, and that someone cared to see Logan as a person, not only the perpetrator of a horrific accident.

"Logan liked mushroom pizza. It had always been his favorite, even when we were kids." A smile crossed Reid's face, and it softened his features. He was looking at me, but at the same time, not *really* at me. "When we were kids, he wanted to be a professional baseball player. He always said he'd play for Cleveland, and for a while, it looked like he had a shot of getting there. Did you know he broke the state record in pitching?"

"No, I hadn't heard that."

"I forgot for a moment that you're a bit younger than I am."

I grinned. "Does it matter?"

Reid stared at me for a beat, and the air changed between us, as if it had suddenly become charged. I liked it and wanted more of it.

"Being young isn't a bad thing," Reid finally said, before he broke my gaze. "Anyway, Logan was like a hero here in Allen when we were in high school. He might have been our father's son, but he had his own... celebrity status. No one held him accountable for the factory closure, or blamed him for it, because he was such a superstar. People always talked about him, as if they were going to get a slice of Logan's success once he hit it big, once he got out of here." Reid's face fell. "But then he hurt his shoulder during the state championship. It turned out that he tore his rotator cuff and had to have surgery at Cleveland Clinic." Reid snapped his fingers. "And that was it."

"That was what?"

"The end." Reid got up from the hallway bench and peered into his coffee mug. "Looks like I'm out. Are you sure you don't want some?"

"Actually, yeah, I will take a cup."

We were growing more comfortable, and I wanted to hear more about his brother. He spoke about him so reverently, in an almost worshipful tone. Reid might have been the older Powell, but he held his brother in high esteem, even with all that had happened. It amplified his immense loss.

We moved into the kitchen, and he fixed me a cup of coffee with a splash of half and half. I sat at the table, and he sat in the seat across from me.

"Have you ever seen *Pulp Fiction*?" I asked as I waited for the liquid to cool.

"A long time ago, when it came out."

"I caught it streaming about a year ago." I sipped my drink. "There's a whole part about silence and comfortable silence." A nervous laugh escaped my lips. I wasn't normally awkward around guys, but things felt different with Reid. I wanted him to like me as much as I was starting to like him, but it occurred to me that the usual ways I might flirt with someone might not work in this situation. So, there I was, clumsy, awkward, and unsteady in his presence. "Just a few minutes ago, I was thinking we're pretty good at that. The two occasions I've sat in this kitchen, we've had a comfortable silence."

He eyed me. "You've been in this kitchen more than two times. Three, considering the dinner and the breakfast during the snowstorm."

"No, no, no, no." I shook my head. *God, I am so horrible at this.* "The first time I was here didn't count. I didn't expect to stay longer than a few seconds, and I was caught off guard. So of course, we didn't have comfortable silence then. But the next day… and today…" *Stop talking, Tarryn. Stop talking, now.* "I'm just pointing out that it's nice. I don't have that with a lot of people."

"I don't either." He wrapped both hands around his mug and regarded it. "And you're right. Comfortable silence is… good."

"Not a lot of good in your life, huh?"

"No, not at all."

Something about his tone of voice made my heart break a little. He needed someone on his side, and I wanted to be that person. Maybe I already was.

"Tell me the rest of your story about Logan," I murmured. "What happened after the surgery?"

"It's… it was a common thing. Happens to a lot of people." Reid looked up from his coffee. "Logan started taking pain killers, and when he needed more, he went to a doctor two counties over, who wasn't much of a doctor at all." Reid sneered. "A man who was arrested for running a pill mill."

"Pill mill?"

"A clinic totally based around writing prescriptions for opioids. Doctor Gregory Miller was the guy's name, and he pleaded guilty a couple of years ago to writing thousands of scripts for patients who needed them to get their fix. Addicts." Reid spit out the final word. "Miller only took cash, which at the time wasn't a problem for Logan."

"Oh my God." I struggled to process what he'd just revealed. "So, your brother was a victim, too, in a way…"

"No, not totally. *No.* Don't put it like that." Reid shook his head. "People around here don't know that Logan got his pills from Dr. Miller, and I don't want them finding out about it, okay?"

"But they might feel different about him if they knew that."

Different about you. Different about your family.

"Logan was an adult, and he was accountable for his own actions. What happened the day of the accident was his fault. *My* fault."

"I just—"

I bit the inside of my lip. I didn't agree with his line of thinking, but Reid sounded so adamant about it that I sensed there would be no convincing him otherwise. Still, I filed the information away. It might be useful later.

"What happened after he stopped getting the pills from Dr. Miller?" I asked. I knew I was prying, but I had a feeling that no one had ever asked Reid's opinion, or how much he suffered because of what his brother did. *Still suffers.*

"He turned to the street. Started stealing, and dealing a little too, when he wanted extra cash. He started making more demands. Everything he did went toward fueling the addiction"

"Oh my God," I whispered. "I feel like I can guess exactly where this is going."

"Because it's a total cliché." His shoulders slumped. "I tried to get him help. I swear it. I put him in rehab three times. It never took." His voice broke, as if the weight of the conversation had taken over, and as if he couldn't bear the heaviness of losing the battle with his brother's addiction. He hung his head in his hands. "By the time of the accident, he was a ghost of his former self."

"Good grief."

"On the last day of his life, he told me to go fuck myself. That he didn't give a damn what I thought. Those were the last words he ever spoke to me."

Neither of us spoke for a while.

"I'm sorry," I said, saying it so he'd know I was still with him in the room, someone cared about him, someone *heard* him. "I'm so sorry, Reid."

He lifted his head. "You don't have to say that."

"But I mean it. I really do." I could see how much this hurt him, how large a burden he carried. It had to be unbearable. It had to be lonely. He needed someone to walk this road with him. *I'm willing to do it.*

I thought about this for another minute. And then, I reached across the table for his hand.

Reid's fingers had a mix of rough and soft patches. The nails had been clipped but not manicured. A spray of freckles dotted the top of his hand, and a large callous filled the space on his palm between the middle and ring fingers. I laced my fingers with his.

He didn't pull away.

It was a simple gesture, a moment of friendship, a way to let him know that someone else supported him, and that even though we had just met, I was willing to be there for him. The heat from his hand warmed my fingers, and an electricity pulsed through me as I realized just how much I wanted to connect with him, how much I wanted to get past what kept Reid Powell from letting anyone get close. It wasn't that he was handsome, or smart, or that his family had once been prominent and influential.

Reid Powell felt things deeply.

He was like a wounded lion, licking a cut that would never quite heal. And I wanted to help him learn to live with the scars.

"Thank you for telling me about Logan," I said. "I know it isn't easy to talk about him."

"I've thought about leaving this place for good a thousand times, Tarryn. I was even gone for a while after Logan's funeral. But…" He looked away.

"But what?"

"You wouldn't understand."

"Try me."

"I made promises to my dad. I told him… he wanted me to not give up on this place. It was his dying wish… but I don't know if *they* want me. And if I can't forgive myself, should I expect them to?"

I studied him, thoughts swirling in my head.

"I have an idea," I finally replied. "And this one just might work."

CHAPTER SEVENTEEN

Tarryn

Dinner with Carter *was* definitely a date.

I knew it. Carter knew it. How could it not have been? We were both dressed for it. I wore a black sweater dress with over-the-knee boots and carried a year-old Marc Jacobs handbag that I'd snagged from an online auction site. Carter wore a pair of pressed khakis and a blue button-down shirt that did little to hide the muscular remnants of his football days. I caught a whiff of cologne when he hugged me at the front door.

But we drove to Youngstown in silence, and it wasn't a comfortable one. *Does he feel that too?*

Agreeing to go out with Carter was a mistake, a big mistake, and I knew it the second he shut the passenger door of his Nissan. The entire way to the restaurant, I searched for ways to let him down easy. I needed to tell him that while I liked him, I wasn't interested in him as more than a friend.

But how?

Vincenzo's Italian Bistro occupied a small retail space near Youngstown's central business square. The restaurant had a small, brightly lit sign outside, and a hodge-podge of tiles on the walls inside. Candles sprouting from wine bottles decorated the tables. A sign on the back wall said Vincenzo's was the longest continually operating restaurant in the city.

A host led us to a center table and explained some specials for the evening. Carter ordered two glasses of red wine when the server arrived and insisted that we try the best northeastern Ohio's Caprese salad.

"How often do you come here?" I asked after we ordered pasta bolognese and veal parmigiana. "You know the menu backward and forward."

"My grandparents used to bring my family here every few months. This was back when Youngstown had a more active downtown. They would make a big deal about it." He laughed at the memory. "I thought that Youngstown was a really big place."

"It's my first time here. To downtown I mean."

Carter's eyes widened. "Really?"

"When I used to visit Dad, he didn't take me to Youngstown. He's not a city guy."

"Does Youngstown still qualify as a city?"

I scoffed. "Sure, it does."

"Don't tell the national media or the politicians." Carter grimaced as he drank some red wine. "They always act like Youngstown is a small town."

"I wouldn't pay attention to them. They only come here during election season, so they don't really know." I sipped my own drink. "Besides, I think part of the region's problem is how it perceives itself. People think they're left behind, so it becomes their reality."

"Well, thanks, Pollyanna."

Heaviness set in around us, the weight I often felt whenever I talked with people from my dad's hometown. They might enjoy life a little, and even escape their reality for a few stolen moments, but that was all it ever was—moments. Real life always hovered, waiting to snatch them back to the absoluteness of their situation.

"It's going to be okay," I replied, thinking about the conversation I'd had in Reid's kitchen. I knew I couldn't confide in Carter about it, or elaborate much, but I wanted my tone of voice to imply there might be something around the corner. "Despite how it looks right now, there are still things to be hopeful about."

"Small things, Tarryn. We need *big* things."

It was hard to argue with that.

The Caprese arrived, an explosion of mozzarella cheese, shaved arugula, olive oil, and bright red tomatoes. The food overflowed the plate, and for a moment, neither of us spoke. We dove into the appetizer, and I enjoyed the chance to eat well-prepared, delicious food.

"I think they're right," I remarked after the third mouthful. "This probably is the best Caprese salad in the area. Maybe the whole state."

"They've always served it like this. No changes at all. My grandparents demanded that we order it every time we came here."

I scarfed down another bite. "I think it's the mozzarella that does it."

"Wait until we get to the bolognese." His mood seemed to lift. "Big chunks of bacon."

"Anytime bacon is on the menu, I'm all in."

Carter's phone rang just as I was about to add to my comment. The ringtone pierced the restaurant. Carter took the device out of his back pocket while grimacing. "I'm sorry, I thought I put this on silent, but—"

"What?"

"It's my sister." In a nanosecond, a deep frown divided his forehead. He held up an index finger. "I'm sorry. I have to take this." He tapped the phone screen and put it to his ear. "Hey I... what?... oh God." His eyes widened. "Valley Medical? Okay, yes. I'm on my way. I promise... thank you. Tell her to hang on."

"What happened?" I asked when he ended the call.

"Laura's in the hospital." A sigh escaped his lips, and it almost sounded like a sob. "We have to go. *Now.*"

CHAPTER EIGHTEEN

Reid

Long after Tarryn left him, he thought about what she'd said during the conversation in the kitchen. She was right in a lot of ways. If he walled himself off forever from the community he loved, nothing would ever change. She'd echoed a lot of Walter's sentiments. And while Reid didn't necessarily believe they were completely correct, the statements came from the two people he probably trusted the most in life right now.

Their opinions had to count for something

That evening, he got in his truck. Reid drove around Allen and its outskirts once more. He didn't know why. He simply felt an urge the prowl the streets, looking for slivers of life he missed. If he followed Tarryn's advice, he wouldn't be able to do that much longer. He'd have to start living in the daylight, instead of existing in the darkness, using shadows for cover.

Reid parked at the town square and watched patrons come and go from The One-Way Tavern. They bundled up against the relentless cold and hugged each other as they walked in and out of the bar. Through the large glass windows, red-faced patrons clicked beers and played darts. TVs flashed with various college basketball games.

And despite the setbacks, the people of Allen tried to press onward.

He admired that about them; he always had. No matter what they experienced in life, no matter how fragile the bonds of their community had become, the people around him still tried to stick together. It was stubbornness mixed with resilience.

And that *also* had to count.

Sometime after seven, he drove to Powell Steel's old lot. On the edge of town, only a rotting shell remained of its former glory. After his father closed the business, the creditors erected a large chain fence around the property, and a giant padlock across the entrance. The metal rusted a long time ago, the lock was now gone too. The front gate swung open, begging cars to come in that never had.

Reid pulled his truck into the parking lot and shined his headlights at the old headquarters. The beams punched through the crumbling bricks and illuminated the opposite end, which backed up to Redbird Estates.

He kept the engine running as he studied the building for almost an hour. He wasn't sure what he was looking for, or if he'd find it in the cracks and jagged edges. He stayed anyway. Time passed.

Reid closed his eyes; he could almost see Powell Steel as it once was. He could smell the glistening steel, sawdust, and sweat that came with a hard day's work. Reid remembered the deep creases around his father's mouth, and the pride in his smile as he clapped a hand on his son's back and telling him that one day all of this would be his and Logan's.

A promise his father hadn't kept.

Reid opened his eyes. Yes, his father liquidated the business at the first sign of real trouble. Yes, he'd opened his golden parachute as CEO and left the town in the dust. And yes, that had been the start of Allen's downward spiral.

But no, Reid didn't have to stay on that path. Tarryn was right. The future wasn't decided. Things could change. And he could be the reason they did.

If he just had the courage...

After a few more moments, Reid drove the car around to the back exit on the property, which emptied out onto the streets that made up Redbird Estates. He pulled the car into the shabby mobile home lot and rolled through the ragged, broken streets of hookups that had once been billed as state-of-the-art affordable housing. It was still cold enough for everyone to stay inside, except for the occasional fight that spilled out of front doors and onto small decks that encircled the entrances to the trailers.

At the end of Sparrow Street, a chill ran up his spine.

A rusted, late-model Chevy Impala was in front of the last unit in the ragged cul-du-sac. The front screen door to the trailer flapped open, and Reid had a straight line of sight into the front room. The car door also hung open, and the emergency lights blinked a desperate warning.

He slammed on his brakes.

Is that a woman's arm?

He peered closer at the door and willed his eyes to focus. *Shit.* It hung limp and lifeless, as if the last surrender flag on a failed mission.

Reid got out of his truck in a flash. He barely had time to park the vehicle before adrenaline took over. He knew an emergency when he saw it, and the wretched feeling in the pit of his stomach told him that if he didn't act fast, he would have *more* than an emergency on his hands.

He'd have a death.

No. No, he wouldn't allow that to happen. Not this night. Not while he had breath in his body.

Reid raced to her side and then recognized her immediately. Laura Monroe. *Carter's younger sister.* He cringed. Hadn't he told her to straighten up? To stop screwing around with men who were little more than boys and drugs that offered only dead ends? She hadn't listened. She'd ignored him. And now... now—

You don't have time to worry about that now...

She was breathing, but the push and pull of her lungs hardly registered on the fingers he put to her mouth. Her eyes were closed, her body as limp as her arm. And a needle stuck out of her left foot, near her ankle. She'd needed a fresh vein to do her damage, and she'd found it, cold weather be damned.

Did he even have to guess what she'd used? Heroin, fentanyl, something else? They were all the same in his mind. All dirty, devious idols people worshiped to hide from the troubles in their daily life. Logan had been the high priest of this religion.

But he'd be damned if he would allow another human sacrifice.

Reid sprinted to his truck. In the months after Logan's death, he'd gathered whatever weapons he could in a desperate attempt to fight the demons he sensed wanted to rob his town of its existence. He'd prepared for revenge, but never had much a of a chance to use what he knew.

He yanked the kit from his glove box and opened it as he ran back to Laura's side, assembling it as he went. *She can't die. No. She won't die tonight.* Not from the cold. Not from the drugs. Not on his watch. When Reid reached her side again, he tilted her head back, shoved the Narcan up her nose and gave the device one vigorous push.

"Come on, Laura," he said to himself a much as to her. "Come on, stay with me."

She came to in a foggy gasp. One moment, Laura was a frozen, lifeless zombie, and the next a panting, sweaty ball of confusion. He moved away from her before she saw his face and he took his phone from his coat pocket.

"Two twenty-eight Sparrow Street," he told the 9-1-1 dispatcher. "There's been an overdose."

She lay in a heap in the driver's seat when he drove away, but he knew she was alive. She gasped and gurgled as her body processed the extremes. Good enough for him. She didn't need to know who'd stepped in to pull her back from the edge. She'd make it, and that's what mattered. Her kids wouldn't lose their mom. Laura Monroe had another chance.

He passed the ambulance on his way out of Redbird Estates.

Tarryn

I'd never seen the aftermath of a drug overdose before. Just snippets on TV, which always seemed blown out of proportion or taken out of context. Never in real life. *Never* like this. This was an alternate reality that I wasn't equipped to process.

Laura occupied emergency exam room three of Valley Medical Center, and when we arrived, she was sitting up on the bed drinking water from a Styrofoam cup. Apart from her drawn face, sallow skin, and haggard eyes, nothing gave away the fact that she'd come within a few moments of losing her life.

But Carter had warned me it would look that way.

"I'm surprised they took her to the emergency room," he had said on the way over, as he drove ten miles over the speed limit on the highway between Youngstown and Allen. "Must be because of the cold."

"Wouldn't they have taken her anyway?"

"No. Most of the time, they don't around here. If they took every OD in Victor County to VMC, the doctors would never treat anyone else."

"But didn't she almost *die*?" I gripped the car door handle. Holding on to it helped some of the stress fade away. Some. A lot remained.

"She did."

"God, I'm so sorry, Carter."

"The paramedics take too many of these calls." He'd gritted his teeth. "She's damn lucky. The other times she's been given Narcan, I've found her in the bedroom, or a day or so afterward."

"Other times?"

"She does this a lot because she doesn't care about herself." He slapped the steering wheel and cursed. "Laura likes the high. If she's close to death, that means she got the good stuff. Junkie logic."

Now, as I stood in the doorway of emergency exam room, I didn't know what to say. I didn't know how to comfort him. Anything I considered saying sounded hollow. The fact was, Laura looked terrible. Whatever high she'd chased had taken away several thousand more breaths of her life and wiped away years she'd have on earth. But I knew from her frown she couldn't see that.

She might *never* see that.

"You're lucky you're not dead," Carter said.

"Whatever. You're so dramatic. They should let me go home," Laura insisted. It was a weird juxtaposition. She sounded angry, but she also looked half asleep. "I'm not sick."

Carter snorted. "I'd beg to differ."

"I won't do it again."

"No one believes you, Laura."

She stared at her brother. "Why are you always treating me like I'm five years old? I'm not a child."

"Well, you sure as hell act like one."

"There you go again. Always blaming me for everything. Aren't people allowed to make mistakes? Or do we always have to be perfect, just like you?"

Carter shook his head. "You sound really grateful for someone who just got Narcan. If they hadn't found you, you'd be dead."

"I *am* grateful," she muttered as she crossed her arms. "But it's a shame the Narcan stole my ride."

Carter let out a long sigh. "You're turning into nothing but a junkie."

I stared at the two of them as they argued. This was awkward. This was a window to a private world. This was a family in crisis. And a huge part of me wanted to leave the hospital, wanted to make myself un-see it.

I shouldn't be here while they're falling apart...

"Maybe I should go," I tried. "We've had a long night."

Carter blinked at me as if he'd just remembered I was there. "No, Tarryn, you don't have to leave yet."

"Really, I think—"

"Who are you?" Laura studied me.

"Tarryn Long." I stared back at her. "Don't you remember me? It's been a long time but—"

"Oh yeah. The prosecutor's daughter." Her eyes grew wider. "Carter, you didn't tell me you're *dating* someone."

Carter held up a hand. "That's hardly the issue here. You are."

"I'm not an issue. I'm your sister." She frowned. "And God, my head hurts."

"I'm glad you're feeling better," I said, choosing to ignore her interest in whatever relationship she perceived I had with her brother. "We were very worried."

Laura drank some more water. "I'm perfectly capable of handling myself."

"Bullshit," Carter retorted. "You almost froze to death tonight, along with taking that crap." He set his jaw and narrowed his eyes at her. "Thank God my niece and nephew were at their father's house tonight, so they didn't have to see this."

"Screw Darren. He never loved me anyway."

"This isn't about your problems with Darren, Laura." Carter shot me a look and took a seat in the metal chair across from Laura's bed. He looked weary and heavy, as if the stress of this moment threatened to break him into a thousand pieces. "You need help. And rehab."

"I don't need any of that. I'm *not* addicted." She glared at him. "But I will tell you something. When I was there, in the car, someone was there with me."

"Who?" His eyes bulged. "Did they give you the drugs, because I swear—"

"They didn't give me the stuff. Don't jump to conclusions." She stared off into the distance, and I guessed she was trying to remember the events of that horrible evening. "But someone came up, just as I closed my eyes. A man." She knitted her eyebrows together. "Yeah, that's it. Older than me, I think. But I swear he was there."

"Oh my God," Carter murmured. "If he did something to you—"

"I don't remember. It's all pretty vague."

I need to leave. I shouldn't be here. This is a mess, and I'm like a voyeur, watching their pain...

I cleared my throat. "I should probably go home." I stopped leaning against the door frame and zipped my coat tighter. "It's getting late." I fixed my eyes on Laura, who couldn't have weighed more than ninety pounds. "I'm glad you're here, and you're safe. That's the most important thing."

Carter stood from the chair. "Well, wait, let me at least take you home."

"No, it's okay." I took my phone from my pocket. "Don't worry about me. You have bigger things in your mind."

His face fell again. This night had gone epically wrong and was far from what I guessed he'd planned when he'd asked me to dinner at Vincenzo's. I felt a twinge of pity, but I also took the evening's events as further evidence that Carter and I probably didn't belong together at that moment. He needed stability in his life, and I couldn't offer him that.

"I'll walk you out," he added in a heavy voice.

"Thank you."

We walked to the waiting room exit just off the main emergency room, passing rooms of people with stricken expressions. And when we reached the hospital entrance, I felt about as heavy as he looked.

What a freaking night.

"This wasn't how I expected this evening to turn out," Carter said when we got to the automatic doors. "I'm really sorry."

"Don't even think about it. I'm just glad your sister is okay."

"For now. But who knows when she will do that again? I can't trust her." He shrugged, and his shoulders slumped. He looked tired, and older than he did when he picked me up that evening. "I can't babysit her either. She doesn't want that."

"It will all figure itself out."

But I didn't believe my own words. They were weak and useless in the face of all he was dealing with at that second. Carter and his sister had complicated problems, and the answers weren't obvious.

We stared at each other for a few breaths.

"I'm going to call Nora," I finally said. "She should still be at the house with Dad, so maybe she can come get me." I punched her contact on my phone and she picked up on the second ring. After a quick conversation, she agreed she could be at the hospital in a few minutes. "See?" I gave Carter my brightest smile. "You don't have to worry about getting me home." Then I bit my bottom lip. Carter looked so burdened. I hated that. "You need to think about Laura. She should be your top priority."

He rubbed the back of his neck and glanced in the direction of the emergency exam rooms. "I've tried so hard. You don't know the things I've had to do just to keep her alive."

"You're a good man and an even better brother. I can see how much you care about her." I stepped forward and put a hand on his arm. "I know you've done a lot."

"Thank you." He scrubbed his face with his hand. "Goodnight, Tarryn."

"Goodnight, Carter," I replied, just as Nora pulled up in her Jeep Wrangler. "I'll check in with you tomorrow."

I gave him another reassuring smile before I trudged out into the cold. The wind whipped my face, and the temperature had dropped since our arrival at VMC.

"Do I even want to know what brought you here?" Nora asked as she drove down the slope from the hospital property to the street.

"You probably don't, but I am sure you can guess."

"Hmm." She clicked her tongue a few times. "Since you were out with Carter, and I picked you up at the hospital, I'm going to take a wild guess." She stopped the car at the red light and looked at me. "Laura."

I nodded.

"Goddamn it. I saw her the other day at the Get-N-Go gas station out on State Route forty-five. The one a few miles north of here. She was running some scam to people to give her money. Probably so she could get money for her fix." Nora propped her elbows on the steering wheel and dropped her face into her hands. "And now this—"

"I haven't seen someone after an overdose before. It's scary."

Nora scoffed as the light changed from red to green. "The worst part is, most of the time, people don't care that the Narcan saved their life. It's like they're pissed they're still breathing."

We fell silent for the rest of the ride home, but when Nora parked the car in the driveway, I turned to her. "I'm glad you're taking this weekend off. Two days off in a row. That's a first."

Nora laughed. "True."

"You deserve it, Nora. No words can really thank you for all the effort and time you've given Dad."

"Thanks." Her eyes were puffy, and her shoulders bowed. "Maybe you were right, Tarryn. Maybe I should have left when I was younger. If I had, maybe I wouldn't be so sad all the time."

She wasn't the only one who was sad.

CHAPTER NINETEEN

Reid

He threw up when he arrived home.

He didn't even make it inside the house. Instead, he'd pulled the truck into the detached garage when the wave of nausea he'd suppressed on the drive finally overtook him. He opened his door and puked onto the driveway.

In a way, the purge felt good. It was like a reset, and that night needed one.

Using Narcan on Laura made him feel helpless, and that stood out to him. He hadn't expected to feel that way about saving a life; that hadn't been the point. The Narcan was supposed to help him fix problems, to give him a way to make sure people didn't end up like Logan. Narcan was supposed to be his ally.

But that night had highlighted how sad the situation in Allen really was, and how deep the problem really went. And that made things feel worse.

He wiped the back of his hand across his mouth. *Pull yourself together. You helped her. That matters.* He knew that, even as he felt some of Laura's pain transferring to him. She was still young and had once been beautiful. Before—long before the accident, and even before the factory closed—Reid remembered her as a feisty second-grader with mud on her shoes and a crooked smile, who stood up to bullies on the playground and wanted to be just like her older brother, Carter. Laura had been a bright light at Allen Elementary, the kid whose magnetism drew people toward her.

Was *that* Laura still somewhere inside the shell of an addict that she was now?

Reid didn't know.

After a few more deep breaths, he got out of his vehicle and trudged across the property to the house. He had five more Narcan kits in the bathroom cabinet, and in the morning, he'd replace the one in the truck. If he needed to do it again, he'd be ready.

He was upstairs before he knew it, and fell asleep on top of the bed, too tired to pull off his clothes and get under the covers.

That night, he didn't dream.

Tarryn

Finally, with Nora off for the weekend, I had the chance to take care of my dad by myself. I knew it seemed almost selfish to relish the moment, but I did. I'd given up college and moved to Allen to be with him, but we'd scarcely had any time to ourselves. Nora's near constant presence had often made me feel useless around the house, and while I more than appreciated her help, I wanted to feel like I had a part in my father's recovery too.

So, I got up early on Saturday morning, prepared scrambled eggs with low-fat yogurt, then took a tray with breakfast to his room. He was awake, and he was looking at the morning light that streamed through the windows.

"Breakfast in bed," I announced. "The royal treatment."

He managed a half-smile. "I know… you. You're… enjoying this."

"What's wrong with a girl wanting to take care of her dad?" I set the tray on the bed then helped him sit up straighter in the bed. "Yogurt with fresh strawberries and three eggs with cheese. Just how you like it."

"You have… whole day… planned?"

"Yes." I moved the tray to his lap. "When we're done here, we're going into the living room to work on your hand exercises. After that, we'll practice walking around the house with the cane. Gonna get you back at that deer blind next hunting season or die trying."

He snorted. "Saw three... other... day... one... eight pointer."

"Well, take that as a good sign."

I took the fork off the tray and guided a bite of scrambled eggs toward his mouth. I knew he didn't like having people feed him, but his fingers still didn't cooperate the away he wanted. No matter. We'd simply work on it until they did.

"Tired?" he asked after the third bite.

"I am. I got back late last night." I sighed and put the fork down. "You know how I was out with Carter? Well, it didn't go very well."

He frowned. "How?"

"It wasn't his fault. I mean, he was trying. I know he likes me a lot, but I don't feel anything for him other than friendship." I broke my father's gaze and focused on giving him more food, this time yogurt. "And besides, he has a lot going on with Laura right now." I looked at Dad again. "She overdosed last night."

Dad slowly shook his head. He didn't have to say any words.

"I'd never seen an overdose before. I mean, she was alive at the hospital because someone gave her Narcan, and she kept insisting she was okay, but she wasn't. At all." A sob escaped my chest. "Why would she do that to herself? To her kids?"

"People... get... hooked."

"I know." I fed him the spoonful of yogurt. "Carter's angry. And I suppose I understand why."

Dad swallowed his bite before he spoke. "I'm worried."

"About the meeting?"

He nodded.

"Me, too." *Especially after last night.*

"Whole town... getting... pushed... to the brink."

"I know what you mean," I replied as I readied another bite of eggs.

While Dad took a short nap on Saturday afternoon, I decided to call Mom. I hadn't been in touch with her much since I moved to Allen, and I wanted her wisdom about the turmoil. She brought up the Harper Automotive closure before I could.

"Looks like you have immaculate timing," she said. "From what I read online, if things weren't already bad up there, they're now getting worse."

"At least Dad is getting better." I shut the door to my room and threw myself on the bed. My old Jonas Brothers posters still hung on the walls, and a pink gingham quilt covered the queen-sized mattress. "He still needs help eating, but his grip is stronger, and he's more mobile with the cane."

"He's lucky." She clicked her tongue. "I still care about him, you know. I don't love him like I did when you were a kid, but I still care. We did spend almost twelve years together." Mom paused. "And I'm proud of you for putting him first."

"Thanks." I studied the ceiling, recalling the blowout fight we'd had right after the stroke, when I told her that I wasn't going back to Ohio State. "And the promise I made you still stands. I'll be back in school by the fall, at the latest."

"Good, because you didn't get this far just to fall short of that degree. I want to see my baby get that diploma."

"I want Dad to be there too. And he will be." I sat up on the bed. "You know, I didn't know what to expect when I came here, and things have been surprisingly different than I thought they'd be. But Allen is also growing on me."

"It is?" Mom's voice sounded surprised.

"I just want to help people. And I think with a little hope... well, don't the people who live here deserve opportunities too? Don't they deserve a chance at a good life?"

Mom sighed. "Yes, but that place has been on the downslope for a long time, Tarryn. I know you're an optimist, but it also sounds a little naïve."

"So what?"

"So, plenty. The problems there are almost generational. And then you add the accident... I got an alert about some piece from the *New York Times* on my phone, and it was all about how the closure of Harper Automotive is pretty much the end game up there. That they don't have many options."

I considered telling my mom about Reid, and the brainstorm we'd had, but in the end, I decided she wouldn't understand. She didn't see things the way I did. Instead, I said, "They're having a meeting at the community center on Monday. I guess we'll find out more then."

Mom sucked in a breath. "If I didn't know better, I'd say you're falling in love with that place. It's getting under your skin, isn't it?"

"It is. I know things in life happen for a reason, and I'm starting to feel like it was my destiny to come here."

"Just be careful," she replied. "I don't want you to get hurt."

We ended the conversation a few moments later, and I lay on the bed for a while longer, scrolling through Instagram and my other old social media accounts. I hadn't posted anything in weeks, and I realized as I lay there how foreign my feed felt. The mix of posts about parties and images of college life didn't feel the same as they had a few months earlier, when I'd been so focused on making my last semester in college memorable and fun. Things had changed.

No, *I* had changed. And that couldn't have been more obvious.

I was still thinking about those changes on Sunday afternoon, when I laced up my sneakers for my usual run. Dad was napping after a successful hydrotherapy session a few towns over, and I felt confident I could leave him alone for an hour or two while I made up for not running that morning. I left a quick note by his bedside and headed out to the road.

Change was the theme of my entire time in Allen. The stroke changed Dad's life. Harper Automotive's closure would change the region's economic outlook. And now, Reid Powell might have the power to make a change too, as long he as he had the courage to do it. I considered that with every step I took. And once again, I decided to pay him an unexpected visit. If there was anyone I wanted to talk to before a meeting like this, it was Reid Powell.

Why not? He did confide in me, after all. That makes us friends, right?

When I made it up the driveway, Reid was chopping firewood near a pile on the left-hand side of the house. He wore gloves, a knit hat, a pair of jeans, and a gray Henley that outlined his biceps. My breath caught in my throat. The fact was, he was handsome and strong. His body beat out a steady, rhythmic pace as he split the larger logs into smaller ones.

He stopped chopping when I got closer.

"This is a welcome surprise. What brings you here?"

"I was just going for my usual run." *Running, and thinking about you.* I walked a few steps closer. "And... I was thinking about the meeting."

"We're all thinking about that." Heavy breaths pushed out of Reid's chest, and his cheeks flushed. Sweat formed a ring at his collar. "When I need to work off stress, I try to do something with my hands. It helps clear my head."

I nodded at the firewood. "You have more chopped wood than you're going to need this winter."

"Probably, but you never can tell. We'll get at least one other storm before the springtime." He braced one hand against the house, leaned into it, and smiled. "Can't say I'm not glad to see you."

I think that's what he said. His devastating smile—something quite rare—had caused my brain to go on a hiatus. *God, the man was delicious.* "Well... I figured... that's what friends do, right?" *Could I sound more awkward?* "They drop in on each other."

I sent up a silent curse. It was all coming out wrong.

"Is that what we are?" Reid asked. "Friends?"

"Yeah, I mean, after all the time we've spent together over the last few weeks, I think we qualify." I was fumbling for words, looking for something to say, and I wasn't doing it well. And I figured he could tell. "We're... um... we're friends."

"Interesting." He leaned closer, his gaze on mine. He smelled liked pine branches, and it only made him seem more rugged. "What if I told you that I'm not looking for friends, Tarryn?"

"Too bad," I managed. "You're stuck with me."

We stared at each other for a long moment, and I felt something shift between us. *He does like me, doesn't he?* I wasn't one hundred percent sure.

"Let me help you," I tried as I pointed in the direction of the pile of firewood. I kept my eyes locked with his. "That needs stacking."

"It does." He broke my gaze, stepped away from me, and brushed his dirty gloves together. "You can help if you want, as the logs aren't too heavy. I've got an extra pair of these in the garage."

He jogged away to get them, and when he returned, I was beside the large jumble of split logs. He handed me the gloves and we went to work stacking the wood into a neat pile alongside the house. It took about ten minutes, and when we finished, I was out of breath. I felt ridiculous, considering that I ran regularly for exercise. *But I'm also so unsettled around him...*

"See?" I asked between gasps. "Friends help each other."

"They do." He gave me a smile. "They also drink together." He motioned for me to follow him up the back-porch steps. "Come on, I've got some good bourbon inside I've been hoarding for a while."

"Don't you want to save that for special occasion?"

"We're celebrating our newly minted... *friendship*, aren't we?" he called over his shoulder. "Sounds like a good enough reason to me."

I couldn't argue that sentiment. So instead, I simply followed him up the steps.

CHAPTER TWENTY

Reid

Tarryn Long was gorgeous. She was also stubborn, caring, industrious, and determined. He knew all those things about her, and when she arrived at his house that Sunday morning, he wondered how he was going to continue hiding his growing attraction to her. She was like the first flower in a garden after a hard winter, something to be cared for and appreciated for the simple fact of bothering to be there at all.

It had been such a long, cruel frost.

But what was the first thing to come out of his mouth once the firewood was stacked against the house? *"Come on, I've got some good bourbon inside that I've been hoarding for a while."* Admittedly, it had been more than a few years since he'd tried to get a woman he was interested in to consider something with him. She couldn't leave so soon, not when she'd arrived under whatever bullshit reason she'd given him. Tarryn had put more fire in his belly than he'd experienced for years... *I want more of that. I want more of her.*

It was the first time he'd done a mundane task like stack firewood with a woman, and it reminded him of his parents. His mom had been like that. She and his dad had been a team in every way, and weirdly, it was that vibe he'd experienced working alongside Tarryn. Well, it was *one* of the sensations he'd felt anyway...

Plus, the bourbon was good. Part of his father's sacred stash, a curated group that included some of the rarest labels on the market, a relic from a time when his father entertained some of the biggest names in the industry at their old mansion in downtown Allen. Reid had never tasted any of it, but it also didn't make sense to keep it locked away, unable to be enjoyed by anyone.

Good liquor should be shared.

He took the most expensive bottle from the kitchen cabinet, along with two small glasses, also from a group of fancy barware he rarely used. "How do you like your bourbon?"

"Neat," Tarryn replied as she took off her coat. Then she shook her head. "Actually, I'm not really an expert. I'll have it however you're having it."

"Neat is fine with me."

She sat at the table, and he watched her as he fixed the two drinks. God, she was gorgeous. Stunning really, and in the way people sometimes missed. The sharpness in her face blended easily with the soft curves of her body, and she still had a youthful light in her eyes, as if she thought the world could still be conquered and that she would make a difference somewhere.

How goddamn refreshing.

He handed her the drink then tipped his own to hers. "Cheers."

"Cheers."

He downed a shot of the bold alcohol without thinking, and without caring that bourbon was a sipping drink, not a shooting one. She didn't follow his lead.

"I've been thinking about your suggestions," he said. "About what you said the other day."

"Oh really, you have?" She drank a small taste of bourbon. "This is good, by the way."

"It should be." He sat at the table. "Not that I really care about quality, but my father was one of those people who did. As a kid, when we went to places like Cleveland or Chicago, he liked to take us out to whatever fancy restaurant he considered worthy at the time. He'd always order an expensive bottle of wine. And if it wasn't perfect, he'd send it back." He shook his head. "It's a shame he wasn't as particular about the business as he was about all the benefits he got from it. If he had cared, maybe all of this wouldn't have happened."

"Maybe not," she murmured, and he heard it in her voice again. She felt sorry for him. He didn't like that. It was the last thing he wanted from her.

"You really think this will work?"

"What other choice do they have? I don't think anyone else has any ideas, and certainly not the ones you do."

"That reminds me." He stood from the table. "Give me a second."

Reid disappeared for a moment, and when he returned, he carried an armload of binders and files. He placed them on the table in front of Tarryn. "This is it—what I was telling you about the other day. The work I did on my thesis, the business plan, all of it."

"Oh, wow." Tarryn opened the first binder and flipped through a few pages, scanning the index of what he'd written. As she did, a piece of him cringed. He couldn't remember the last time he'd shown this to anyone, and he wasn't sure he could bear it if she rejected it.

But then she smiled at him. "Are you aware of how awesome this is?"

"Well, it's a plan, but that doesn't make it a good one." He sat down at the table again, feeling an invisible weight roll off him. She hadn't turned this down. She still supported it.

"This is going to take a lot more than a bunch of paperwork." He laughed a little bit, regarding the mountain of pages. There must been a thousand of them, some yellowed and frayed, and a few printed from an ancient dot-matrix printer. "After the accident, I backed this all up on a hard drive I keep in a safe deposit box down at the bank. I told myself I'd throw all these hard copies away one day, but I never did."

"Powell Advanced Robotics. Good name. I like it." She studied a few more pages. "No, I *love* it. We can do this."

We. He grasped his empty glass with both hands. "I've been thinking about that too. You're the first person in years who has given a damn about me, outside of Walter."

"Because you've carried the burden of your brother like a boulder in front of you. Because you've let that keep you away from everyone else." Her eyes softened. "Things don't have to be that way. The people in this town can change."

He cocked his head, studying her, and admiring the optimism in her words. "But what if they dismiss this? Call it a stupid idea?"

"They won't. They *can't*."

"You're not going to let them, are you?"

She shook her head.

He smiled. "That's one of the things that I like about you, Tarryn. Once you dig in, you dig in."

"I do."

He circled the lip of his glass with his finger. "And by the way, I've also been thinking... I could use some extra help, when the time comes."

"Help?"

"If—when—we open up the space again. It's going to take a whole team, and I'd like for you to be a part of it."

Her mouth dropped open for a split second. "You do?"

"You believe in this idea. And I think..." He cleared his throat, feeling a knot of nervousness grow in his stomach. "You told me you were studying marketing, and—"

"When did I tell you that?"

"The first night you were here, when you were delivering the groceries."

She cocked her head. "I did?"

"Yes." He grinned, silently proud of himself for remembering so many little facts about her. Perhaps that was one of the things he'd been doing all along—memorizing

Tarryn. "We have to have you on the staff. *I* have to have you on it."

He knew Allen wasn't exactly a fantastic place for a woman like her to land. Tarryn might have family ties to the town, but it was more than economically depressed. It was economically shattered. She'd have other, better options elsewhere. But if his plan worked, Reid knew he had to have Tarryn by his side.

He got up from the table, poured himself some more bourbon, and sat down again. "You can do public relations, or social media... or... tell me you will at least think about it."

"I will," she said, but her voice didn't give anything away about her final decision. "And thank you for the offer, Reid. That's very kind of you."

They drank the rest of their bourbon in silence, and when they finished, he wasn't ready for her to go. Time with her was... always too short. *Damn it.*

"Thanks for this," she said when their glasses were empty. "It was some of the best I've had."

"And how much bourbon have you actually had in your life?"

"Not much." She smiled and got up from the table. "It's not my first choice. But this was good. I liked it more than I expected."

She walked over to the large sink in the corner and he followed her. When he arrived beside her, he put his empty tumbler in the sink next to hers and rinsed them both. Tarryn's hair smelled like orange zest.

God, he loved that smell.

"Well, friend." She faced him after he turned off the water. "I suppose I should head out. It's almost five, and Dad's expecting me home soon."

"Don't want to keep him waiting."

"No, I don't."

Her words were slower, with more space between each one, and he wondered if she was elongating the moment, just like he was. Reid drew in slow, heavy breaths, knowing he wanted to end this farce. He wanted more than friendship, he wanted her.

"I should probably walk you out," he said.

"Yes, you probably should," she replied, her words slower still.

Neither of them moved.

An eternity passed, and the liquor flowed through his blood, heading up his veins. He needed her. And she seemed to feel it too...

"I keep thinking about the other night, Tarryn. Your hand in mine. I liked it." He looked toward her hands and then he slowly caressed the back of them. *She's soft, like silk.* He wanted to touch her face and see if it was as silken as her hands. *I want to touch every part of her.*

"I liked the other night too." Her eyes crinkled around the edges. "A lot, actually."

Her reply felt like an answer to his unspoken question. Whatever he'd been feeling for her, she felt something similar. Reid's focus shifted to her rosebud lips, and he was unable to resist them anymore. He took a step forward, ran his fingers up her arm to her neck, touched the satiny skin there, and then lowered his lips to hers.

For so long, Reid had kept himself away from everyone else. He'd denied himself any human connection. He felt he didn't deserve it, that he was unworthy of the pleasures in life other people took for granted. Shutting himself away had felt like a justifiable punishment for the sins of his past and the transgressions of his family.

But as his lips melted into hers, he felt a tremendous, deep sense of relief. The stress in his neck unwound, and the pain he carried on his shoulders seemed to fall away, as if he truly was putting down the heavy bag of regret he'd carried around for forever. Her lips were sweet, supple, and waiting for him. As their kiss deepened the connection did too. His fingers tangled in her hair, and his body pressed against hers. He didn't want the moment to end, and he couldn't remember the last time he'd laid himself so bare.

"You're so beautiful," he murmured against her lips as he felt her move in sync with him. "The most beautiful thing I've ever seen."

He kissed her chin, then her jaw, then finally nipped and sucked her neck. She moaned as she moved closer to him, and while he knew she was enjoying it, she couldn't have enjoyed it as much as he did. Touching her was like feeling the softest blanket around his body and tasting her was like eating the finest chocolate in the world. He wanted nothing more than to drink her in, and here she was, letting him.

"I don't let people get close to me," he said between kisses as his lips reached her hairline next to the shell of her left ear. "But I want to change that with you."

"Me too," she replied between heaving breaths. "I *do* want to know you, Reid Powell. I see you, and I want nothing more than for you to let me in—to let me be with you."

He pulled away slightly to let his gaze reconnect with hers. "Are you sure?"

"Yes."

Their mouths came together again. Every kiss laced with passion and pent-up need; electricity pulsed through his body with every touch, every movement.

But then he saw the clock on the wall behind her.

"I'm sorry," he said as he broke one of their deepening kisses. "It's past five."

Her face was flushed, her lips swollen. Her balled fists clung to his thick sweater. She wanted to go further. Every cell in his body knew that. But they couldn't. Not today.

"I don't want your father to worry," he said as he pushed aside his feelings. "He's been through enough."

"I'm a big girl." Her voice was coated in desire. "He won't mind if I'm a few minutes late."

"No, I've already kept you too long." *And what I want right now would take more than a few minutes.* He took her hands in his and met her gaze. "This is just the beginning of something, not the end."

"I hope it's the beginning," she whispered.

"I promise you, it is."

It was as far as he could go, as deep as he could let her in. Part of him still worried she wouldn't like what she'd find if she saw the real Reid. She'd recoil in horror at some point, and it would all become too much. Letting her in was a risk, and he wasn't sure how much his heart could allow.

So, even though he wanted her, he led her to the front door, down the porch steps, and to his truck. He folded her into the passenger's seat and pushed down the pang of sadness coupled with the reality that she was about to leave him again.

I'll take you home," he said.

"I can run home, Reid; it's okay."

"No, I kept you longer than expected. I'll drive you home. And I'll see you tomorrow night," he said, then he walked around to the driver's side and got in. "At the meeting. I'm coming."

"You're the only one who can make the case. I think it's a great idea, but it's your idea, not mine."

He leaned over to her and gave her a quick, reassuring kiss, one that said what had just happened in the kitchen wasn't a one-time thing. "Since you put it that way, I'm definitely coming. No matter what."

When she smiled in return, warmth filled his heart. *God, he'd been alone for so long.*

As he turned out of Springhill Lane, Tarryn said with conviction, "Reid, have faith in yourself. I believe in you." And he knew how lucky he was that she stumbled down his driveway on a cold, blustery night not long ago.

"That means more to me than you can imagine, Tarryn. Thank you." Her dad's place wasn't far from his home, so it only took minutes to make it there. When they pulled into the driveway, he gave Tarryn his phone number, and she gave him hers. He laughed at the fact that they hadn't exchanged them before. And because he couldn't resist, he leaned across the console again and took her lips for a longer kiss, one that left them both breathless. *One I hope communicates to her how precious she is becoming to me.*

Reid watched her walk up the steps to her dad's, looking a little dizzy. She turned back once to smile and wave, and that was when he knew he was done for. *So beautiful. So pure. I want her as mine.* Once home, he entered the foyer, and for the first time in a long time, the house didn't feel so cold.

CHAPTER TWENTY-ONE

Tarryn

The night before the meeting, I couldn't sleep. I lay in bed and stared at the long hairline crack that crossed the ceiling of my bedroom. I tasted Reid on my lips and felt him in my heart. I replayed what happened in the kitchen and focused on my favorite parts. I wanted to memorize the pain in his eyes and the way his body felt when he wrapped his arms around me.

I also prayed.

I wasn't religious. No one in my family was. I hadn't been raised in a church, and I didn't make a habit of calling on a higher authority in my life. But if there was ever a town that needed prayers, it was Allen, Ohio. Allen needed more than that—it needed a miracle. And I hoped the meeting the following night might help them see a chance for one. Besides, things couldn't get much worse than they already were.

The meeting was on everyone's lips the next day at Country Market. Customers talked about it as they waited for slices of deli ham and asked each other if they planned to attend while standing in line for checkout. A few asked me if I would be there, then they weighed in on what they thought would happen. Most didn't expect a lot to come out of it but figured they'd show up anyway. Marlena mentioned it in passing as we restocked the eggs, and Herbert talked about it while mopping the floor in the stockroom.

After work, I drove home and found Dad in the living room, already dressed in a pair of khaki pants, white collared shirt, and navy jacket. He looked more like the prosecutor he once was, and the sight of him made my breath catch in my throat.

"What?" he asked when he saw my shocked expression.

"I didn't know if you'd be well enough to attend." I bit back a smile. "And I'm glad you are."

"Nonsense… not missing this."

I sank into the aging couch across from him. "Everyone talked about it at work today, and I think the whole town is going. Think anyone will offer a solution to this mess?"

It was a leading question, but I wanted to hear his answer anyway.

His face fell. "Wish I could."

"You're too hard on yourself, Dad. You always have been. That's one of your biggest faults." My mind raced as I wondered if I should tell my father anything about Reid's plans for the evening. "Listen, I… what if I told you I think there's going to be something big happening to-night?"

"Meaning?"

I looked into my father's eyes and leapt. "Okay. Over the last few weeks, I've become friends with Reid Powell."

His jaw slackened. "What... about... Carter?"

"Carter and I will never amount to anything. There was something missing. He seems... so angry. Deep down."

"But... Reid Powell, Tarryn? He's—"

"He's not what you think." I held up a hand to keep him from speaking. It felt good to at last admit I'd had contact with him, even though I wasn't giving Dad all the information about what had transpired between Reid and me. "Not as *bad* as you think, is what I mean. He's... he's kind. Compassionate. Intelligent too."

My father grunted. "You know... what... I think."

"I do. I know what everybody thinks. And trust me, so does he." Exasperated with how poorly I was handling this, I let out a deep sigh. "But he's not what you think. I promise."

"Some people... can't be fixed."

"He wants to help. He has ideas. Dad, I've seen the plans. Before his brother died, he wanted to start a new business, one that might be better than Powell Steel."

Dad looked like he wanted to interject, so I held up a hand to stop him from speaking. "He thinks the community can forge a new path with applied manufacturing." The words raced out my mouth as I tried to argue my case in front of the man who'd once put murderers in prison and had taken down drug dealers. "He still has the family money, you know—what was left of the Powell fortune. Reid's living on their property, hardly spending any of it. But he thinks he can use it as the nest egg for the business."

"I don't... know," Dad managed with slow yet firm words. "Allen will have to trust... him."

I moved forward until I teetered on the edge of the couch. This town was hanging by a thread. In a matter of weeks, unemployment would skyrocket, and that would have ripple effects across the city. I sensed it, and I knew other people did too. Uncertainty hung in the air and permeated our surroundings. This community, this region, needed a miracle.

Even one that came from an unlikely place.

"He's going to come to the meeting. He's going to try. I've talked to him about it, and think I've managed to convince him it's the only way." I searched my father's face, looking for confirmation that I was right. But like a good lawyer, he gave away nothing. "People have to forgive him. They can't hang on to what happened for forever. Life is too short."

Dad's expression softened. "You're wise beyond... years, Tarryn."

I shook my head. "Call me an eternal optimist. But I do think if they give him a chance tonight, this might work. What other choice do we have?"

Dad answered my question with a slow nod. "He was... the smart one of... the boys... when he was... younger."

"That's why I think this will work," I replied, then I sent up another silent prayer, this time hoping I was right.

Cars crowded the civic center lot, and the meeting still had twenty minutes before it started. I wove Dad's SUV through the lot, then settled on fighting for a spot in the overflow parking lot across the street at the First Methodist Church. People streamed into the building, and we ran into folks from every section of town and beyond.

"The whole... county's here," Dad muttered to me as Nora and I navigated his wheelchair up the short ramp to the front door.

"I'm not surprised." I had one eye on my father and the other on the crowd. I was scanning it for Reid, looking to see if he'd arrived. Before we left the house, I sent him a text telling him to meet me in the lobby before the meeting began, but he hadn't replied. I hoped to God he wouldn't lose his nerve at the last moment.

We found seats near the front of the room, and I removed the aisle seat so Dad's wheelchair could go there. He greeted a few people by name and introduced me to others, but I was distracted and barely focused on the parade of people who wanted to wish Dad well and ask how he was doing.

Come on, Reid, don't chicken out...

The meeting began a few moments after seven, and as it did, a fresh rush of anxiety coursed through me. I hadn't found Reid in the crowd. He hadn't replied to my texts. And the worst part was, I couldn't let anyone know how much it bothered me.

Glen Johnson, the mayor, sat in the front of the room on a metal folding chair, flanked by other members of the

Allen town council, and a few other county officials. A podium with a microphone was next to his seat. Glen wore a rumpled business suit and a cracked pair of leather loafers. The American flag and the Ohio flag rounded out the disappointing, disheveled display. When the room filled up, a few uniformed deputies from the county sheriff's office directed the overflow crowd to the community center basement, where they said a simulcast of the meeting would play. Media outlets from Youngstown and Steubenville ringed the back of the room, their camera equipment poised to record every moment of the evening.

I choked down a lump in my throat as Glen called the meeting to order. Every minute that passed reminded me of the precarious situation the entire community faced. And the drawn expressions on people's faces only further highlighted how much Allen and Victor County needed to catch a break. No one smiled. No one laughed. They greeted each other in hushed voices and gave each other knowing looks.

It was a mess. *This town is a mess.*

"As you know, I've called this meeting so we can have a community-wide forum about the closure of the Harper Automotive plant a few communities over. For many decades, that plant has been the major employer in this town."

"Practically the only employer," called a male voice from the back of the room.

"The only good one," said another.

A few people nearby murmured in agreement. Marlena folded her arms, and her husband said something in her ear. Herbert sat beside them with a stone-faced look. Next to my dad, Nora's expression was unreadable.

"Now, point of order please." Glen banged a gavel on the podium. "I would ask that you hold your comments to the end of this meeting, so we can present our efforts to handle this situation to you, and so we can provide updated information." He slammed the gavel once more for emphasis. "There is no sense in talking over each other, and I assure you, there will be plenty of time for public comment and questions."

The crowd rumbled in answer, then quieted as Glen began to go over what the town leadership understood would happen to the plant. Most people already knew the details but hearing it all again was painful. Very painful.

No, the plant would not reopen under any circumstances. No, there would not be a chance to appeal the decision. Yes, the decision had been complicated. The company would move the jobs from Ohio to a new plant in Mexico, despite offers of tax breaks and incentives from the state. Employees would receive a minimum of two weeks' pay, along with tiered severance benefits based on how long someone had been employed with Harper.

"I've talked to several emergency assistance groups in the state, and they are willing to provide short-term needs for the folks who find themselves with a strapped budget. Food banks, baby care, toiletries, etc. And a few local banks in the county are willing to give zero interest loans to those who need them."

"What am I going to do about my mortgage?" Mrs. Needleman threw up her hands. "It's seven hundred bucks a month."

The man sitting next to her grumbled a reply to her question. He pulled his arms together. They might as well have pulled on the tension in the room. If this place was a balloon, it was about to pop.

With my eyes still focused on Glen and his depressing presentation, I fished my phone out of the crossbody purse I'd forgotten to take off when I sat in my seat. I unlocked the phone and searched for a reply from Reid. Still nothing.

Maybe he isn't coming. Damn it. He better not lose his nerve.

I tapped out another message asking where he was then folded the phone onto my lap and waited for a reply. As I did, Glen opened the conversation to pre-approved statements from the community. A handful of people from the general crowd filed to a microphone on the far side of the room. None of them looked happy.

One woman explained that she had worked for Harper since graduating from high school, and she worried she wouldn't be able to find anything in the region that would pay as much as she made at the plant. A man said he didn't want the quality of the county's educational system to further degrade once people inevitably left the area for new jobs. Another said he didn't know how he'd pay for his mother's monthly diabetic medication once he lost his steady job.

And so on. Each comment made me feel worse than the last.

My phone finally buzzed during the fifth and final statement about the impact of the Harper closure. I flipped it over.

I'm here. Outside.

When the last comment wrapped up, I turned to my dad. "I have to go to the ladies' room," I whispered. Then I got up from my chair and slipped out of the event space.

CHAPTER TWENTY-TWO

Reid

He almost didn't go to the meeting.

Despite Tarryn's assurances that it would be okay, and he'd be able to convince the community he could lead them, he still didn't feel as comfortable with it as he wanted. Something nagged at him, pulled at his deepest nerve, wavering his resolve to attend. He knew the people of Allen. They were part of his DNA, just like his ancestors, and he knew they were often proud and stubborn to a fault. They'd thrown him out years ago. Branded him like a leper. Why would they change their minds now?

That question and a hundred others thundered around in his mind all Monday morning and into the afternoon. It permeated through every mundane chore he did to pass the time before the meeting. Why? Why would they ever accept him? Why put himself out there like this?

Reid still wasn't ready to go when Walter arrived at the house around five thirty with fresh canisters of paint and a few other items he'd picked up at the hardware store in Stansview. Instead of finding him dressed and ready, Walter walked in the house through the back door and saw Reid slumped at the kitchen table, a half-drunk glass of bourbon in front of him.

"What's wrong?" Walter set the paint and other bags near the door. "You okay?"

"Yes." Reid raised his head. "No."

Walter crossed toward him, ripping off his thick gloves and unzipping his puffy work coat. "Come on. You look like hell." Walter sat in the chair opposite Reid. "You're pale and clammy." He pointed at the bourbon glass. "Don't tell me—"

"You don't have to worry. I'm not like Logan." Reid studied his longtime employee and wondered if he wanted to confide in him. Walter might think it was a dumb idea, but he *had* said to stop sulking and start living. *Fuck it. Maybe he'll listen.* "I'm supposed to go to the meeting tonight."

"At the community center?"

Reid rubbed the back of his neck, struggling with how to catch Walter up on what had transpired over the last few weeks. "Tarryn Long, Peter Long's daughter has become a... friend over the last few weeks, and she talked me into going. She wants me to give a presentation tonight, to talk to the people about what ideas I have for how this town can do better."

A smile cracked Walter's seasoned face. "That was Tarryn's necklace, wasn't it?"

Reid ignored the comment. "She says I have to do this; she thinks the town needs me, and I need them."

"Agreed."

Reid shook his head. He didn't like Walter's conviction. His family had done nothing but fail over the last two generations. Why should he be any different? "I'm not sure I can do this. I might be a Powell, but for fuck's sake, that's not much of a legacy, is it? That's not much of anything, except pain and heartache. My father—"

"Your father." Walter let out a rueful laugh. "*Your father.*"

"What?"

"Do you want to know the truth?"

"The truth?" Anxiety pooled in Reid's stomach before racing up his back. Did he? He wasn't sure. And could he handle it if the truth was something worse than he'd imagined? He gulped. "Yes."

"Your father was a good man, Reid." Walter pointed at his chest. "And believe me, I should know. I might have worked for him, but over time, it got to be so much more than that. It was friendship."

"You were *friends*?"

Walter nodded. "Almost his right-hand man. Your dad told me a lot of things over the years, especially things that had to do with the business."

Reid wrinkled his nose. "Which he sucked at."

"That's where you're wrong." Walter sat back in the chair, but it seemed to Reid that he was almost growing, getting larger, with every word he spoke. "*Everyone's* wrong. They think he wasn't good at business, and he made the company go bankrupt on his own, but it wasn't that." Walter fixed his eyes on Reid. "Are you finally ready to hear this?"

Reid's mind raced and his heart skipped in his chest. What had Walter been hiding all this time? "Go for it."

"Your dad had a silent partner who backed the business with a twenty-percent stake. At first it went well, and the company flourished. But that man started speculating on real estate, and he used his shares of Powell Steel to get credit where he needed it. Then those investments went under and"—Walter snapped his fingers—"Powell Steel collapsed too."

If he hadn't known Walter for so long, Reid would have sworn the man was lying. That he'd made it all up. But he wasn't. Everything in Walter's expression said he was stone-cold serious. Still, Reid gaped at him. *None of this was my father's fault? None of it at all?*

"I don't understand," Reid managed. "Why didn't you tell me this before?"

"Your dad made me vow I wouldn't. He was too embarrassed, too ashamed. He felt like he'd been the one to misread his business partner, so he was ultimately to blame. *His* last name was the same as the company, so he needed to take responsibility. And he did."

The memories flooded Reid's mind. He saw snippets of the past like photos in a flip book. His mother, crying at the kitchen table. His father, on the phone late at night, making calls from his office in a clipped, frantic tone. The invisible heaviness that appeared over him, cricking his back, slumping his shoulders, and turning him into an old man in the space of one night's sleep. The whispered comments Reid heard him make after the closure to the people who had once been his employees. That day in the parking lot of Country Market when he saw his father pass twenty dollars through a handshake to a former foreman.

Had he read his father's legacy wrong this entire time?

Yes, I did. This town was wrong about him. I was too.

Reid stared at Walter for a long time, still in disbelief. His father wasn't a bad man, wasn't a loser who messed up his family and his town through his own misdeeds. He was... he was *human*. And he could be forgiven.

"Don't you see?" Walter finally said. "You're a Powell. You gotta stand up and be a man." He beat his clenched fist on the table. "Your father's memory deserves it. And your family does too."

"You're right," Reid said, clarity washing over him for the first time in a long time. "You're absolutely right."

"Of course, I am." Walter stood. "Come on, let's get your best suit out of the closet. You need to make an impression at this meeting, goddamn it."

Reid followed his employee—*no, his father's friend*—through the house to the master bedroom. He felt the energy around him changing, as if he'd been trudging through a thick fog, and now the sun had burned it off. "Are you planning on coming tonight?" he asked.

Walter turned at the doorway. "Nope."

"Why not?"

"Because I can't do this again." Walter moved through the bedroom. "I was there when your father announced the closing, and it was one of the worst days of my life. Then he died, and it felt like one of my family members was gone. After that, your mother, and Logan...

If you fail… I don't think I can take it. Better to not be there at all."

He yanked a suit jacket from the back of Reid's closet and handed it to him.

Reid answered Tarryn's texts as he strode across the overflow parking lot. It seemed to him that every person who'd ever known him or his family was at the community center. Lying in wait, and yet not really knowing what was coming.

"I thought you were going to bail," Tarryn said when she reached him in the middle of the lot. "I figured I would have to go to your house and drag you here." She caught the back of his head and gave him a quick kiss. "Are you ready?"

He was. Tarryn's confidence in him was a true comfort, but her kiss? A brief touch of affection to a starved man? Magic. He pushed the last vestige of nervousness away. He *was* ready. More than he could tell her at that moment. "Let's do this."

"You were born to do it."

Tarryn dusted some lint off the black woolen coat that went with his suit. He hadn't worn it since Logan 's funeral, and the fabric felt scratchy and heavy against his body. He didn't like the stiffness of it, and he realized once again just how much his exile on the property had changed him.

He looked down at her, trying to drink in some more of her infectious optimism. She believed in him. Walter believed in him. And most of all, he was starting to believe in himself.

"You know what? As a kid I used to think that one day I'd move to one of the big cities, like Cleveland, maybe, and command the Powell empire from there, like some big-shot executive with a driver on call and a laptop as my third arm. I never envisioned pleading for my life in front of the very people who ended up scorning me" He spread a hand. "It's funny how things turn out. But I'm ready, Tarryn. I'm ready for this."

"You have a lot of things say to them." She nodded at the front door. "And they need to hear it."

"What's the mood like?"

"Kind of like being at a funeral for the town. Everyone is under one big shadow," she said. "They could use a hero. And that's you."

"I don't know about that." He gave her a weak smile. "But let's get in there."

She took his hand, and they strode across the lot, then into the building. The lobby and hallway were empty, but there was no mistaking the sharp voices that came from behind the closed doors of the assembly hall. The meeting had moved on from the public testimonial to the question and answer session.

"Okay, Reid Powell," Tarryn said when they arrived at the double doors to enter the main assembly room. "You said you wanted to change things. That you wanted a fresh start for all of this. Well, here it is."

Anticipation rushed up and down his spine. She was right, he *had* asked for a fresh start. Begged for it. Prayed to God that one day he'd find it. And now he had the chance he'd wanted. This was his moment to prove to everyone he wasn't another deadbeat Powell, another disappointment that would only be a shadow of the legacy his family had once commanded.

Time to reclaim my place. Now.

"Should we just walk in?" he asked.

"I think we should." She gave his hand a reassuring squeeze. "But let's wait until they're transitioning from one speaker to another. They don't expect you to be here tonight, so it's going to be something of a shock." She tightened her grip on his hand again. "No better way to do it than just dive in."

"You're right," he said on a deep exhale. "Makes it simpler."

And about two minutes later, they got their chance.

Tarryn

I don't know what I thought I'd see once everyone realized Reid Powell was there, and I was with him. I knew they'd be surprised. Confused. Perhaps even upset. Their emotions were up, and their guards down. It would take them a moment to process it.

But when we pushed through the doors, every person in the room turned to face us. Every eye fixed on us. Every scowl came our way. So did every frown. A fire code sign on the far wall said three hundred forty-one people could sit in that room. I estimated that at least that many people were there, if not a few more, I held Reid's hand as tightly as I would hold a piece of gold, or the key to a priceless treasure chest.

I was in this with him, and there was no going back.

"I know a lot of people have something they want to say tonight," I said as we made our way up the center aisle. "But I think there is one voice that really needs to be heard, and it's the voice right next to me."

"Excuse me, Miss... Miss Long, what are you doing?" Glen called from the podium. "Those who wanted to speak submitted their requests in advance. They filled out forms." He held up a stack of white papers I hadn't realized were there. "And we need to—"

"Please excuse her, she's a little enthusiastic." Reid stopped in the center of the room, and I followed his lead. "She encouraged me to attend tonight, and she's right. I needed to be here because I love Allen as much as the rest of you."

I didn't stop the grin from crossing my face. *Finally*, Reid had found his voice. He was about to show people what I already knew—he wasn't an outcast or a throwaway person. He had worth. And they needed him.

"I have an idea. A plan." He slowly turned in a circle, addressing everyone who sat in proximity, and even those who didn't. His voice grew louder, and I heard the certainty in every syllable he spoke. The TV cameras in the back of the room craned toward him. "A long time ago, my family let this town down. We lost our way, and for that I am truly sorry. I know I might have to spend the rest of my life atoning for their mistakes. But that doesn't mean I haven't found the path back to what is really important."

"This isn't a meeting to talk about the Powell family misfortunes," said a man in the back row wearing a red trucker hat. "We've had enough of that over the years."

"That's fair. You're angry. You've been angry. And I get that. I would be too. I have been," Reid replied. "Pain has almost become your lifeblood. But tonight, I come to you to present solutions, not problems."

He was sounding like a leader. Like a man worthy of the family name and the success that had once come with it. I had to marvel at that. It was exactly what I'd seen the night he helped me with my car. Reid was a man of principles, and anyone there that night would have heard it.

I glanced at my dad and saw what looked like the hint of a half-smile pulling at the good side of his mouth. *Good. If Reid can convince him, he can convince anyone.*

"When my brother died, I became the sole heir to what remained of the Powell family interests. And for years, I've sat on that money." Reid wrinkled his nose. "I thought one day I'd use it for something, and I even drew up a business plan for what I wanted to do." He reached into his jacket and pulled out a folded piece of paper. "I have it all written down right here, and more of it at home. I've held on to it, hoping one day the time would be right, but never fully believing it would come."

He unfolded the paper. Every eye in the room remained fixed on it. *On him.* "This is exactly what I'd like to see happen in this community, and what I know we are capable of here in Allen. The best part is, I'll back it all.

With the Powell capital. And everyone who wants a job can have one."

"What kind of jobs are you talking about?" asked a woman closer to the front row.

"I'm glad that you asked." Reid flipped the paper around. "I'm talking about advanced robotic manufacturing. It's one of the major international trends, and there's a high demand, but we can do this in the US and not take the work offshore."

A few murmurs of what sounded like approval passed through the crowd.

"I want to reopen Powell Steel on the old site and retrofit it as a high-tech factory that makes engines we can sell to Europe and other places." Reid smiled at the crowd. "It might take some retraining but—"

"Nope, I don't want to be *retrained*," said a man who stood up from his seat in the third row. He wore a faded T-shirt embroidered with the Harper Automotive and a dirty white ballcap. "I don't want to waste my time learning skills that *might* be marketable."

"Just hear me out," Reid replied. "I think you're jumping to conclusions before you've heard the whole proposal."

"I don't need to hear anything from the likes of you." He took off his hat and wiped a sweaty brow. "For where I stand, nothing a Powell ever did in the last twenty years has brought us any good. Why should we trust you now?"

Oh, God. My stomach twisted.

"Please calm down," Reid said, his voice more measured than I expected it to be. "As I said before, you have a right to be upset, and I would be if I were you, too—"

"You're *not* me. You have *no idea* what it's like to be me, so don't even pretend that you can understand."

A few people in the room grumbled in agreement with the man's sentiments, and as they did, my stomach lurched some more.

"You're right. I don't know what it's like to be you; I haven't lived your life." With his voice still controlled and calm, Reid addressed the rest of the room, which he still held in rapt attention. "But I *do* know what it means to be from Victor County, and to call Allen home. We work hard here, and we're some of the most loyal people in the country. We lend a hand to our neighbors when they need it and—"

"Like the hand your family extended mine?" a different male voice called from the back section of the room.

I recognized it and turned around to find Mike Reeves standing. Even though we had never spoken, I recognized him instantly. His twin boys had died in the bus accident. They were only seven years old. Second graders. And Mike had been one of the most visible parents in the news coverage of the story, always willing to give an interview. The passing years had aged him—a permanent frown creased his forehead, the corners of his mouth turned down, and his leathered skin highlighted large bags under his eyes. I remembered at that moment how he'd worked for a long time on the assembly line at Harper Automotive.

He was going to lose his job. Another one of life's indignities. Bad luck could have been this man's middle name.

Shit.

"Jeff and Jason never leave my thoughts," Mike added. "The rest of the world might forget about my boys, but I never will."

"I haven't forgotten them either," Reid replied in a low voice.

"But why should we trust you?" asked a woman I didn't know well, who I'd seen a few times at Country Market buying the same set of groceries every two weeks. "You might still live in the community, but you don't *care* about us. You live on that property out on the state highway, and you've stayed away. You don't know what we're really going through."

"Yeah," chimed in a different voice. "You don't know us."

"I'm not willing to invest in another Powell scheme."

"Not worth it."

The chorus of voices came faster and louder. People nodded at the comments and seemed emboldened as more people voiced their dissent.

"This family is good for nothing, anyway. All they do is take, take, take."

"He's probably the same as his father. A lazy idiot with no good ideas."

"We need to move away from steel anyway. It's brought us nothing but heartache."

"You know how those Powells are. We've known it for decades. A bunch of greedy bastards."

"All they did was sell the company and hoard the money. Then his brother spent his inheritance on drugs."

My attention swung from the crowd, to Reid, and back again. I didn't know what to do. I didn't have a plan for this. Their words were sharp, raw, and almost violent.

Can't the people in this town see that this is their best option?

"Wait," I cried out as the cacophony grow louder. "I don't think you're being rational—"

But I shouldn't have even tried to protest. No one was listening to me. They were tied up in their own anger, their own pain, and their own dissatisfaction with solutions they felt would fail them.

And then one voice spoke louder than the others.

"From where I stand, we have only person to blame for what's happened here. And folks, he's standing right in front of us."

CHAPTER TWENTY-THREE

Tarryn

The vitriol I heard behind the words made me shudder, as did the owner of the voice. Carter stood at the end of the aisle near the back of the room, a clear path between Reid and him. And at that moment, the differences between the two men couldn't have been clearer to me.

The crowd quieted down once Carter spoke, which didn't surprise me all that much. He was a pillar of the community, and the owner of the most successful bar in town. If anyone in town had a right to speak at this meeting, it was him.

"You already know how I feel about you," Carter said with a steady voice as he took a set of careful steps toward Reid. "I suppose it turns out that we all can't simply forgive and forget."

Reid didn't reply.

Carter stopped two steps away from Reid, and his attention remained fixed on him. The rest of the people were silent, and that added to the eerie sensation that descended on the room.

Carter studied Reid for a moment, like a tiger sizing up prey. He was the man I knew, and yet, at that moment, he wasn't at all. His chest was puffed up. He stood taller. And something seemed almost dead behind his eyes.

"From where I stand, as I look back on it, we have only one family to blame for the misfortunes of this town, and we all know it. We all feel it." Carter spoke to the rest of the townspeople, as much as he did to Reid. He crossed his muscular arms, still focused on him. "If the Powells had never come to Allen in the first place, we wouldn't be in this hell we're in." He glanced at the rest of the community. "Who agrees with me?"

"We do," chanted a few voices. "We do."

Carter acknowledged the TV cameras, then turned to the crowd again. "Which family took our money, and our labor, and gave us almost nothing?"

"The Powells," shouted a large group in the room.

"Which family stole our lives? *Our children*?"

"The Powells."

"Which family got us addicted to pain killers when we hurt our backs on the job and our bodies gave out?"

"The Powells."

Almost all the people in the room were taking part in the call-and-response now, and it sounded like a bizarre tent rally at a revival, as if Carter was the preacher, and they were the congregation about to be saved from certain damnation. I looked at the mayor. Glen still stood near the podium, frozen, staring at the group.

Do something. Do something...

He didn't move. Carter called out another accusation, and the crowd answered back. He was judge, they were jury, and the list of crimes they wanted to convict Reid Powell of grew longer by the second. Even Dad seemed swept up in it, nodding as if he agreed with at least a few of the charges Carter leveled at Reid.

My God, this is turning into a mob...

I switched focus to the deputies posted around the room. Town leadership had known this would be a contentious meeting and had asked for extra help in handling any outbursts of raw emotion. Surely, they would calm down the gathering, which heated up with every charge Carter laid at Reid's feet.

But they didn't do anything either. They simply stood at their posts, blank faced. That's about the time the reality of it all really struck me. This wasn't just regular anger, a general feeling of animosity. This was systemic rage.

And *they agree with him. They agree with Carter.*

I stepped forward. I needed to do something, or at least try. "Come on, please, let's stop this," I shouted, straining to have my voice heard over the clamor of the crowd. "Everyone is upset, but this isn't the way to handle it."

"This isn't your place, Tarryn," Carter said with barely a glance in my direction. "You're not one of us."

"But I'm—"

"It's okay," Reid said to me, which he accompanied with a hard, knowing look, as if he wanted to calm me down, to get me to go along with whatever he believed he'd be able to make happen next. "You don't have to do this, Tarryn. You don't have to defend the indefensible."

"My sister is an addict," Carter called to the rest of the group. "And we all know that. Like many of us, she has struggled with opioid addiction for years."

A low murmur of sympathy and agreement moved through the room. People could identify with Carter's problems. They had them too.

"She has never gotten the help that she needs, and the other day, she overdosed." He spread a hand. "Do you know how she got started? Where she first got the opioids?"

"I can guess," yelled a man from the middle of the room.

"I'm sure you can." A smirk crossed Carter's face, and that told me he was enjoying this, he liked the command he held over the rest of the community. They were united in their fury, with Carter as their leader. "She got them from Logan. Logan Powell for fuck's sake. He started her on them and got her hooked before she knew it." He pointed at Reid's chest. "She would have done anything for those pills, and she *did* do anything for this good-for-nothing-sack-of-shit's brother. Logan Powell didn't just kill those kids that day. The truth is, he was killing this county long before he got behind the wheel."

My stomach lurched. I wondered if I was going to throw up on the linoleum. I wasn't sure how much more of this bizarre vigilante trial I could take. I wanted— needed—to get out there, and fast.

I need to get Reid out of here too.

"Do you know how Logan got his money? How he was able to live all those years, wreaking havoc on our lives? The cold truth is, *Reid Powell* financed his brother for years. He supported him. Kept him off the streets and enabled him to keep on dealing. Hired high-powered attorneys to get tickets fixed and charges dropped. He's the mastermind, folks. There is only one person we still haven't taken care of in this town. And it's you, Reid Powell."

With that final sentence, Carter closed the space between himself and Reid. Then he balled his fist, swung it, and landed a punch right in middle of Reid's mouth.

A surprised look crossed Reid's face, but he didn't remain off-kilter for long. Instead, he punched Carter back, landing one on his cheek.

That was all they needed.

The two men descended into a fistfight right in the center of the community room. They swung punches and lunged at each other as the crowd cheered them onward, pushing the energy of the room to a frenzy. Carter and Reid struggled against each other—two men evenly matched for a moment like this. Soon, they were a blur of shoves, kicks, punches, groans, and contact, all of which made it impossible to determine who was winning the fight. Not every blow landed its mark, but many did. People gathered around, shouting, taking out their phones to record the melee. My heart raced as I watched, helpless to stop them. And I kept waiting for someone to intervene, for someone else to wake up and realize this was not the way to handle things.

No one did.

I scrambled atop an empty chair and yelled at one of the deputies. He shot an empty stare in my direction then shrugged. *Fine. Screw this.* If he wasn't going to help me, then I'd get someone who would. I pushed through the tight crowd and ran to Glen's side. He was the mayor. The town leader. He'd step up.

"You have to stop this," I pleaded. "You have to. Now."

"I can't." Glen kept one eye on the melee. "They need to fight this out."

"Not here, not like this." I gave the scuffle another frantic look. It wasn't getting better or slowing down. It was getting worse. "*Please*, this isn't the way to settle something."

I didn't understand why I was the only one who seemed rational at that moment, why I was the only person who still had a clear head. Fighting at the civic center wouldn't solve any of the town's issues, and if it didn't stop soon, it might escalate further, to something irrevocable.

We can't afford to see what that looks like.

"You're the mayor. The *mayor*," I added, and my voice broke into a sob. I tossed a glance at the melee. "You have stop this. Now. No matter what you think about Reid Powell, this can't go on. Fighting like this isn't going to solve the problem."

He blinked at me. More punches flew. The frenzy grew.

"Please." I almost screamed it. "Please do *something*."

"Okay," he said after another long moment. "You're right."

CHAPTER TWENTY-FOUR

Tarryn

G len raised the gavel and banged four times on the podium. The sound shattered the room, and rose above the fighting, above the mob. "This ends now."

He banged the gavel two more times.

"That's it. I am ordering you to stop. This fight is officially over. No more of this."

The group seemed to wake up then, and people pulled away from each other. Two men separated Reid and Carter, who were now both bloody and bruised. I let out a small sigh of relief. At least the physical altercation had stopped.

"I'm the mayor of this town and I declare this meeting adjourned," hollered Glen over the dying rumble. "This gathering is over, and before there are any arrests, I hereby order everyone in this room to disperse. Gather your things. Go to your homes. Exit this building in an orderly fashion. The deputies are under my orders to take into custody anyone who lingers here past eight forty-five. This public hearing is closed."

A rumble of discontent rolled through the room.

"What did I say? This gathering has ended. Now."

At least Glen *sounded* strong, and he did have authority, but the frowns and crossed arms in the room told me that his decision didn't satisfy many. Still, as they put on their coats and filed out of the aisles, I took advantage of the break and rushed over to Reid, leaving Nora to help my father get to the car.

He nursed a split lip with two fingers and looked like he had the beginning of a black eye. Blood spatter sprayed across his shirt, and his jacket sleeve was torn. He rolled his right shoulder a few times, as if he wanted to stretch it.

"Oh my God." Gingerly, I reached two fingers to his face. "Are you okay? Did you lose any teeth?"

"No, I didn't." He gave me a weak smile. "Also, I don't know if you could tell, but I was winning."

I smiled at his joke, but it didn't do much to assuage my concerns. "That lip might need stitches. Do you need to go to the hospital?"

"You should see the other guy."

He nodded in Carter's direction, and I looked over at him for the first time. He was in slightly worse shape than Reid and like he also might have the start of a black eye. But I realized I didn't recognize that man any more. He wasn't the kind, friendly man who'd asked me to dinner and inquired about my dad. He was a stranger.

I turned back to Reid. "Let's go. I'll walk you to your car."

We caught some nasty looks and snide comments as we walked to Reid's car, but for the most part we were able to make it to the parking lot without incident.

"I don't feel good about what happened," I said on a sigh when we arrived at the driver's side of his F-150. I was close to crying, and struggling to hold it back, to choke down all the raw emotions that night had dredged up inside of me. *We failed, and it's my fault...* "I was the one who encouraged you to come tonight, to lay yourself bare on what you wanted to do, to try to connect with these people again."

"At least we tried."

I took his hand in mine. He winced, and I knew he'd have swollen fingers the following morning from all the punches he threw. "I shouldn't have pushed you to come tonight. That was the wrong idea, and it was too soon for them in there. It was like setting you up for failure."

"You can't control them, Tarryn." He dropped my hand and shoved his deep into the pockets of his coat, which he pulled tighter around him.

"I want them to see how good-hearted you really are."

"Don't worry about me. Worry about them." He jerked his head in the direction of the community center and the dwindling crowd. "And you know what? In one way, it's refreshing. Carter has always wanted to fight me. I don't think he'll try it again."

"Still, I feel so bad."

"I'll be fine. Eventually." His eyes searched my face. "I'd kiss you right now, but I'm still bleeding from this fat lip."

I smiled again. Reid had every reason to be angry and combative, but he wasn't. I marveled at his steady resolve. "I'll come by later, okay? After I get my father home. I'll come by and check on you."

"Sounds good," he said, then a slight frown crossed his face. "Wait, I totally forgot—"

"Forgot what?"

He pulled his clinched right hand from his coat pocket. "This. I forgot this." He held his fist out to me, then opened the palm. "I think this fell off the night of the storm. I never got it back to you."

There, in the middle of his hand, lay my sterling silver monogram necklace, the one with my initials etched into a delicate pendant. I hadn't even noticed it was missing.

"I kept meaning to get it back to you," he said. "And for whatever reason, it was never the right time."

"Thank you," I breathed as I took the jewelry from him. I put it around my neck and took a deep breath, glad I had it. "Thank you so much for holding on to it. My dad gave it to me for my eighteenth birthday. I can't believe I didn't notice that I'd lost it."

"You're the one, Tarryn. The one who changed everything for me. You make me feel alive," he added and got into his truck.

I stood in the parking lot and watched until he drove away.

Dad and Nora were beside his car when I walked up to it a few moments later. He was talking to a few deputies, but when they saw me approach, they excused themselves and moved to another group of people who lingered in the parking lot. Still further away, several television crews interviewed a few stragglers about the meeting and the fight.

"Well, *that* was interesting," Nora commented as I helped her get Dad into the car. "One for the town's history books."

"What? All the forums in Allen don't regularly end in epic fist fights?"

Dad laughed at my joke and Nora gave me a small smile. "He was winning before you put an end to it," she said. "And I'll admit that I liked seeing that happen. Reid has some fight in him, and I'd forgotten that. He's tough."

I straightened Dad's seatbelt. "One of the reasons I like him."

"I honestly have to say, I'm sorry that this community keeps handing him the burden of his family. You can't pick your parents, or your siblings. People have been unfair to him, and I realized that tonight, during all of that screaming." Nora frowned. "They aren't considering the whole picture. It's like they've lost their way. No, *we've all* lost our way."

"I guess raw emotion will do that to people."

"A shame," Dad added.

I nodded, shut the passenger door of our car, and got in the driver's seat. The three of us drove home in an awkward silence, and I used the trip to try to process what I could about what had happened. And most of it, I couldn't wrap my head around.

"I'm going for a drive," I announced when we were home, and after I'd helped my dad get settled into bed. "I'll be back later. I need to clear my head."

It wasn't an entirely true statement, and I suspected my father knew that, but he didn't challenge me on it.

I got back in the car and decided that before I checked on Reid, I would simply drive around Allen, letting the cold winter air and crisp darkness iron out some of the anger, despair, and disappointment I felt.

No matter what Reid did to win their affection and respect, the people in his town wouldn't ever fully forgive him for his family's past transgressions. He would always be an outcast to them, an outsider they would blame for all the misfortunes that occurred. They'd found their whipping boy, and they were going to make sure he got punished. *Maybe forever.*

When I turned onto Main Street near the center town square, I saw a small crowd of men.

They huddled together, hunched shoulders in thick winter coats. They all wore hats to ward off the cold, and heavy boots to keep their feet warm. They talked together in a small circle.

Something about it made me curious.

I parked my car about twenty feet away and watched as they talked. I cracked my window and tried to hear what they were discussing, but I was too far away to make it out clearly.

But then I saw Carter standing in the center. He said a few more things to the people around him, then on his signal, the group dispersed and moved to their waiting cars. Each person got behind the wheel, then formed a line in the street.

When the last car rolled away from its spot, I decided to follow it. And I knew where they were going the moment they turned onto the highway. There was no other explanation. No other reason for their actions.

They were going to confront Reid.

Judging by the residual anger and the stiff, determined way they held themselves, it wasn't going to be with words alone. No other way to see things. Not after what had happened at the meeting.

Oh, God...

As I followed them, I located my phone with one hand and tried to call Reid through voice command. I needed to warn him that they were coming. If he was alone, he deserved a heads-up about the danger that was on its way.

I called him once. No answer. Twice. No answer. Three times. No answer.

By the third try, the panic in my body overwhelmed me. My hands shook as I drove the car. A cold sweat broke out on my brow. A flash of adrenaline coursed up and down my neck.

But he still didn't call back.

Damnit.

I parked the car away from the group, which traveled up to Springhill Lane in a long, snaking caravan. The men didn't notice me. They got out of their cars and moved toward the house, which had several lights on in various rooms.

Instinct told me everything about this. We needed the police out here immediately, so I called 911 before I got out of the car. A dispatcher picked up and didn't sound thrilled or motivated about sending anyone out to Springhill. *Why not? Shit.* I still had my phone in my hand, so I tried calling Reid one more time. "Pick up. Please pick up. Please..."

Nothing.

I didn't want to reveal my presence to the gang of men, so instead of using the main road to the house, I cut a path through the brush and trees that rimmed the property. I wasn't exactly sure what I was doing, but I kept my attention on the men, fixed on what they were doing so I could recount it later. I sent Reid a text as I crept closer to the house. The men gathered in a group, said a few grumbling phrases, and then one pushed forward up the steps to the front door of the house. I took a few photos and some video.

Then I hid behind a large tree and peeked around it to watch. One man screamed Reid's name a few times. No answer for him either.

And then I heard a hissing whisper.

"Tarryn."

CHAPTER TWENTY-FIVE

Reid

W hen Reid got home from the meeting, he changed his clothes, laced up his snow boots, bundled himself inside a heavy parka, and decided to go for a walk around the property. Sometimes, long walks helped him clear his head. Gave him the perspective he needed. Kept him from drinking too much.

More than anything, he needed clarity tonight.

Reid was in the cemetery when the caravan of cars arrived, standing in front of the side-by-side graves of his father, mother, and Logan. His fingers were bruised. His face bloodied. His neck hurt.

And he was praying.

He'd tried to help Allen. He'd tried to do what his father wanted. He'd *tried* to bring about change.

But Reid had failed. Epically and utterly failed.

Whatever happened next for this community wouldn't come from him—it had to come from something bigger than he could provide. Reid knew that now. They didn't want his help, didn't want to see him as any different from the people who'd let them down in the past. He wasn't the savior they needed. He never would be.

In a way, he guessed he should have expected the mob to come. The confrontation between Carter and him was in no way finished, and Reid knew it. Carter wanted another shot to prove he was a better man, and Reid could have guessed by the way the deputies reacted to the initial fight that the story wouldn't end at the community center.

And of course, Carter hadn't arrived alone. He hadn't left this moment to only himself and Reid. He'd brought reinforcements. A lot.

This is it.

Reid crept through the trees as he watched the group circle together. He took cautious steps, his eyes on them the whole time.

Fuck. I should have brought my gun.

He balled his hands in his coat pockets and remembered that he'd thrown his phone in there on the way out the back door. A call to the police might not do any good, but at least he'd know he made the attempt. He took the device from his pocket and unlocked the screen.

Tarryn's phone calls and messages greeted him.

Damn it, he'd placed his phone on silent before the meeting, and he hadn't remembered to flip it back. Each message grew more frantic than the last, and by the last one, he was confident that Tarryn was on her way to the property, or even there at that moment. Then he saw her, hiding behind one of the largest oak trees in the forest on the far side of the cemetery.

"Tarryn."

He called her name in a hushed whisper, before his head got the best of him. He was glad to see her again and impressed she'd followed what looked like a group of broken-ass vigilantes to his house. But he was also scared. If something happened to her, he wasn't sure he could take it.

"Tarryn," he tried again, a little louder. "Tarryn."

She turned her head on his third attempt. "Reid."

She rushed over to him, carefully avoiding the broken branches and twigs that littered the snow, trying to not make noise that might alert the men to their presence.

"Holy shit," Tarryn said when she reached him. She also barely spoke above a whisper. "What the hell is happening?"

He pulled her against the trunk of a thick ash tree and raised a finger to his lips. Then he leaned into her ear. "I'm sure you realize it's Carter and his friends."

She met his gaze and nodded. Her breath was ragged, and her chest heaved. "Reid, I don't—"

"Shh." He gripped her arm. He saw terror in her eyes, and he felt that way, too. He knew Carter's need for vengeance hadn't been satisfied at the community center and he was here for blood. "Keep your voice down."

"I have a horrible feeling about this, Reid. I think I'm going to throw up," she said on a strangled breath.

He pulled her closer, wrapping his arms around her as tight as they could go. Whatever happened next, he needed her. *I won't let her out of my sight.*

"I've never been so terrified in my life," she said, the warmth of her breath stinging the frigid air.

Together, from their place in the forest, Tarryn and Reid watched one of Carter's associates bang several times on the front door, then return to the group with his hands in the air. "Where is he?"

"He's such a fucking coward." Carter stepped away from the disgruntled group. He turned his whole body to the house and yelled, "I know you're in the house, you bastard. Come out here."

"He's *insane*." Tarryn choked on the word. "I don't even recognize him anymore."

"Let's finish this," Carter roared at the house. "Right now, Reid Powell. Tonight."

Carter returned to the other men, and they spoke for a few seconds. Then one person broke away from the group and stumbled to the garage. He shoved his shoulder against it several times until the door broke open on the last heave. He disappeared into the structure and returned with a large canister of gasoline.

"Look what I found." The man held up the can. "I think this will be useful."

A low rumble passed through the men, and Tarryn turned to Reid.

"Oh my god," she hissed. "They're going to burn your house. They're going to set it on *fire*."

She moved as if she wanted to get up, as if she planned to make herself known to the group, but Reid grabbed her arm and pulled her toward him. "Don't go over there right now." He grasped both sides of her face. "What if they try to kill you?"

"What if they try to kill *you*?" she asked.

He put his forehead against Tarryn's and hoped his calm breathing would help her settle down. Settle *him* down.

"Let's see exactly what they're going to do, okay?" Then he took his phone from his pocket, opening the camera application. "And get evidence, of course."

She protested one more time, but when he insisted he didn't want to confront them, she relaxed against him, and he opened the camera application on his phone.

As they watched, several members of the group raided the garage and found more gasoline cans. They broke through the front window and screamed Reid's name. When he didn't answer, they huddled together once more, then broke into groups with the fuel, spreading it across the perimeter of the house. They threw it in the bushes, spread it on the porch, and coated the windows.

This was it, and he knew it—the moment in his life when everything he'd ever cared about, every locked-up memory, every faded remnant of the past would be taken away from him, destroyed in one fateful, irrevocable act. He pulled away from Tarryn and fell to his knees in the snow, overcome with the weight of the sight playing out before him.

"I've seen enough," Tarryn said between gritted teeth. She took her own phone from her pocket and dialed 911 for a second time.

"They won't come." Reid muttered, not acknowledging her anymore, knowing that once again, it was all happening just how he should have expected, helpless to change the moment no matter how hard he tried.

"I don't care what they say. We need help." When the call engaged, she gave Reid's street address. "Get here as fast as you can," she murmured into the receiver. "There's an emergency on Springhill Lane." Then she hung up the phone and shoved it back into her coat pocket. "At least they know about it. Someone besides us knows."

Carter yelled Reid's name two more times and demanded that he show himself. He directed the mob to move away from the house, then grabbed a lighter from his back pocket. "You're a coward, Reid Powell. And I don't care how many ideas you have. We want you gone, and don't *fucking* come back."

With a maniacal laugh, Carter tossed the lighter onto the gasoline. The moment of no return passed in the flicker of a nanosecond.

"No, no—no!" Sobbing, Tarryn fell next to Reid. She grabbed his hand and shut her eyes. "I can't bear to see this happen. I can't take it." She buried her face in his shoulder, crying, stifling her wails in the fabric of his coat. "This is wrong. So wrong."

And it was. But unlike her, Reid watched the fire begin.

The flames moved through the rooms of the old farmhouse, growing larger from the accelerant. The structure was no match for the strength of it, the ancient beams and plaster didn't put up any fight as the fire traveled, taking with it all the antiques, paintings, files, photographs, and memories that Reid had filed away, all the physical pieces of what remained of his family, and his past. Each piece seemed to make the fire grow.

For a moment, it was too much. When the flames punched through the attic and devoured part of the roof, Reid shut his eyes too, knowing with an overwhelming dread that all he'd cared about was gone. He had nothing left. Nothing. His whole world had been destroyed. And then a thought crossed his mind.

The past is over.

Reid opened his eyes. The voice in his head didn't sound like his own, and he wondered for a moment if he'd misunderstood it, if he'd mistaken his own pain for something that simply wasn't there. And then he heard it again, along with different voice in his head, both clearer this time, with a cadence he hadn't heard in over a decade.

You don't need this anymore. This is just a building. It isn't you.

"What do you mean?" he asked as the fire illuminated the night sky and swallowed the left side of the house in a few deep groans. "What do you mean it isn't me?"

The first voice spoke to him one more time.

Rebuild, Reid. Start new from here.

"What if I can't?" he asked.

Tarryn opened her eyes. "What if you can't what?"

Reid didn't answer. He turned his head to the sky. "What do you want from me? What am I supposed to do next?"

And then the thought crossed his mind. The voices he'd heard were right. Here was his chance. He'd have to move on from this, he wouldn't be able to stay stuck in the past anymore. Things would change from here, the fire guaranteed it.

"You're right." He said, as much to himself as to whatever he'd felt moments before. "It's time."

"Time for what?" Tarryn shook his arm. "Time for what, Reid?"

Reid turned his face and focused on her, blinking a few times. "Nothing," he said, as he helped her up from the snow. "Nothing."

As he spoke, his mind was still on the voices, though, and what they'd collectively said to him. *The past is over. You don't need this anymore. This is just a building. It isn't you.*

How many hours had he put into remodeling the Victorian? How much thought had he given to swatches of paint and tile design, and all for—what? How many times had he used it all as an excuse to blot out his grief, as a band-aid that would never fully fix the past?

After this night, he'd no longer have this crutch.

But I have something else. Something better. Someone better.

"Let it go," he said. "Let it burn."

"What?" Tarryn said, her whisper not hiding her incredulity. "*What*?"

"It's okay," Reid moved closer to her, holding her tight. "This is just a building. A personal hell, in a way. It isn't me, and it isn't my future."

"But this is a *crime*."

"It is." He laughed without humor, thinking of the voices in his head, and what they'd said to him in the darkness. He pushed a few stands of hair away from her face and cupped her chin between his index finger and thumb. "But I just want to wipe it all away."

"It shouldn't have to end like this." She pressed against him. "Not with you losing everything. I'm so sorry."

"Don't be, Tarryn. I can't explain it all right now but... don't be sorry about any of this." His fingers moved from her chin to her jawline. "There's more to this night than you realize."

He kissed her, this time ignoring the pain in his lip and the screaming muscles in his chest. He wanted her to know she hadn't ruined anything, that even though he didn't think he'd ever be able to explain it to her, he'd see this night for what it was—the moment when his life began again, when all that had haunted him faded away in the charred embers of what remained of his family's house. And more than that, he wanted to feel just how much she'd changed him, how much he needed her. Reid couldn't understand it, but every time he was with Tarryn, he felt himself thawing, felt the frost around his heart melting away.

It had been so long since someone had challenged him like she did, since someone cared, and he needed this to last for all time—

"Guys, I see him. There's Reid Powell, in the woods," screamed a drunken voice. "And someone's with him."

The words sliced through their moment.

"Fuck."

Reid pushed Tarryn behind him to keep her safe. *She can't be hurt in this. That's not happening.* People were running toward them, and all Reid could think about was Tarryn's safety. He'd fight again, but it wouldn't be for the

217

house burning to the ground behind the approaching men. He had more important things to worry about, and he knew that now, knew it without a doubt. Seconds later, Carter pushed his way to the front of the group.

"I knew you were on this goddamn property." Carter rushed toward Reid with a set of closed fists and a snarl. "Did you not hear me call your name? Why the fuck didn't you show yourself?"

"I was enjoying the little party you decided to throw on my land." Reid replied. "Looks like you're having a good time."

Carter cursed, pulled back his left arm, and landed his fist on Reid's jaw. He stumbled backward from the force as Tarryn screamed for them to stop.

The fight was on. Again.

Reid charged Carter as the fire continued to grow. Flames shot from the wooden Victorian, and the fire lapped at some of the heavy lawn equipment Reid stored near the garage. If the fire department didn't arrive soon, the blaze would spread to the trees, and from there, threaten every acre that Reid owned.

Somehow, the two men fought as if the fire wasn't happening, as if they were alone in a boxing ring, and only one of them would survive. Whatever pent up anger they'd burned off at the community center had reignited. Reid knew Carter wasn't holding back. Didn't have any reason to. Even if it killed him…

And then, just as Carter pinned Reid down with his knees and sat on top of him, a shrill woman's voice cut through the grunts and chants of the group of men who'd followed Carter to Reid's home.

"Carter! Stop!"

A skinny woman with a coat too lightweight for the temperatures pushed past a few of the men. She yelled Carter's name and demanded he stop. When she was ten feet away from Tarryn, she yelped.

"Laura, what are you doing here?" Tarryn demanded.

CHAPTER TWENTY-SIX

Tarryn

"What are you doing?" I asked again.

The commotion of her arrival halted the fight, and both men stared at us. The crowd around us rumbled as well, and out of the corner of my eye I saw the fire jump to the garden shed near the house. *We don't have much time…*

"Why are you here, Laura?" Carter asked between panting gasps. He still held Reid pinned to the ground with his knees.

"I got a text. Heard you'd tried to kick Reid's ass at the meeting, and that you were planning something after he handed your own ass to you instead."

From a distance away, I heard approaching fire engines and their sirens. I exhaled. Firefighters would be here soon.

Thank God.

"This doesn't concern you, Laura."

"Are you kidding me?" With both hands, she shoved her brother in his shoulder. He winced. "You don't get it, do you?"

"Get what?"

She sighed. "Get off him, Carter. Let the man stand up, for fuck's sake."

"No way." Carter regarded Reid. "This motherfucker is the reason things are screwed up. We'll be better off when there are no more Powells in Victor County."

"No," she screamed. "He fucking saved my life."

"What do you mean *he saved your life*?" Carter asked after what seemed like an eternity. He looked down at Reid. "What did you do?"

Laura lunged forward and grabbed her brother's arm. "He's the one who gave me the Narcan, okay? Get off him. *Now*."

Carter followed his sister's orders and heaved himself off Reid's body. "What are you talking about?"

As I moved over to Reid and helped him stand, I kept one eye on Laura.

"A few days ago, when I was in the hospital and I overdosed. He's the one who rescued me."

The entire crowd was silent. I stepped closer to Reid and clasped his hand as I struggled to process what she'd said. *Reid saved her that night. He saved her, and no one knew. Would anyone have ever known?* My grip grew tighter as I pondered the weight of what he'd done. He squeezed back, but kept his attention fixed on Laura.

"You don't need to talk about what happened that night," Carter replied. "It's embarrassing."

"You don't have to keep protecting me. This is the truth." She gestured at the rest of us. The sirens drew closer.

Her words came out hard and fast. "I remember it clearly now. It came back to me the other day, actually, but I couldn't be totally sure." She addressed Reid. "I'm right, aren't I? You gave me Narcan."

Reid nodded. "Yes. I did."

Questions and disbelief rolled through the crowd. Laura ignored them.

"For the longest time, all I could remember was that I passed out in the car. It was a good feeling. The best, really. I wanted it so badly." She said to her brother. "But we all know I came close to dying that night. And I'm not so far gone that I want to die. Not like that." Her voice broke into a loud sob. "Not alone, not when I have kids—"

"It's okay," Carter murmured as he moved to his sister and enveloped her in his arms. "Come on, I've got you."

Laura turned to Reid and said, "It was you in the alley, too, wasn't it? That night with Jimmy... and the payment—"

"It doesn't matter, Laura. All that's in the past. I just want you to get well," Reid answered.

"And I'm not, am I? I'm not—"

"Laura," Carter started, but she held her shaking hand up.

"But that was you, that night, wasn't it?"

Reid nodded. "Yes, that was me."

Carter turned to face Reid, and his face was filled with unmistakable shock. "You saved he*r twice*?" Carter said in disbelief. His anger had abated. His adrenaline and fury had run out. He seemed... empty, as if every morsel of outrage had been stolen. But then he turned back to a sobbing Laura. "Jesus Christ. Oh my god."

As the two of them cried, the firetrucks, paramedics, and deputies finally arrived. About forty feet away from our place in the woods, they parked their vehicles in the clearing at the mouth of the driveway. A few firefighters jumped out of the trucks and pulled hoses to the fire. In the chaos of their arrival, a few people in the crowd decided to flee the scene. No one tried to stop them from leaving.

"They're here," I said as the first sprays of water hit the fire. "They came."

The fire chief ran over to the crowd and asked if anyone was still trapped inside the house. Reid assured him no one was, and then made excuses for the start of it. "It was a bonfire. And we were too close to the house. It's my fault. A total accident."

"Really? Seems like a pretty big accident," the fire chief replied. "We'll have to do an investigation once the hot spots are all put out."

"I don't think that's necessary." Reid clapped a hand on his arm. "Being out here all alone, I stock a lot of firewood, and sometimes I burn my trash." He turned his head as if he wanted to make sure the chief understood his hidden meaning. "I was an idiot, and I started the fire too close to the house tonight."

The chief looked from Reid to the burning house and back again. "I can see that," he said slowly. "But I also don't believe you. Are you sure there is no other explanation for something like this?"

Reid glanced at Carter and Laura. "No, there isn't."

"We might not be able to save much." The chief zipped his fire-retardant coat a little higher on his neck. "Hard to get adequate water up here, and some of the hoses are freezing."

"Save what you can," Reid remarked, then he led me back to Carter. He still held his sister, and they stared at the flames. He must have seen the panic and confusion on my face. "It's all going to be okay, Tarryn."

"Back hom—I mean back in Cincinnati, any fire department would launch an immediate investigation," I said, careful with the volume of my voice, so that only he would hear me. I thought of all the arson stories I'd seen on the local news over the years. "They wouldn't simply accept a story pulled out of thin air."

"I know." Reid took my hand in his and squeezed it. He moved his mouth to my ear. "Carter committed a crime, and I get that, but right now I just want this all to go away. Anything to help this night be forgotten. I'll… I'll try to explain later."

"Fuck, man," Carter choked, forcing our attention his way. "Your home. Fuck, I'm sor— His shoulders slumped. "Had no idea you saved her life. And I don't know how to thank—"

"Don't thank me. The addiction took everything from Logan, Carter. I hate that his addiction *still* takes. There wasn't Narcan to save him back then." He shrugged. "I started carrying it around. Just in case."

I angled closer to Reid and marveled at him. Who was this man? I could hardly believe a guy like him existed, and that despite everything, he would still want to do good in the world. This was—this was a *miracle*.

Reid nodded at the remains of the house, where the firefighters still struggled to contain. "Maybe this was a blessing. Maybe this needed to burn down for me to realize it's time to give up the past."

"I feel so ashamed," Carter whispered. "I held this whole town's misfortunes against you, and I am truly sorry."

Reid focused on him for a moment. "I accept your apology. If I were you, I probably would have done the same thing."

Carter studied him for a few breaths. "No, this isn't right. Apologizing is not good enough. Not even close." He turned to Laura. "Take care of yourself, okay? I won't be able to look after you or the kids anymore. I won't be able to help you."

"What?" Laura's eyes grew wide and she started shaking. "What are you saying?"

He pulled her toward him, gave her a long hug, and pressed a kiss onto her forehead. "I love you, Laura. Don't you ever forget it." He squeezed her one more time. "I love you."

"What? I love you too, Carter."

He studied his sister's face for a second more. "Are you hearing me? Do you understand me? I will always love you. Whenever you're scared, I want you to remember that. Promise me, Laura."

"I... I promise."

And then, without another word to any of us, Carter pushed away from his sister and walked to the deputy closest to us. I couldn't hear what he said, but it didn't matter. A few seconds after they spoke, Carter was in handcuffs, being led to the nearest police car.

"Carter, stop. Not like this, Carter," Laura screamed. "Carter, please."

Laura wailed as the officer pushed Carter into the back of the vehicle, but her cries didn't alter anything. He'd made an epic mistake, and his life wasn't the only one changing in the wake of the fire. As I watched it all unfold, a lump grew in my throat. This night had taken something from all of us, and I couldn't believe it. Carter gave his sister one last long look as the deputy turned on the car.

"Oh my god," I managed, my words thick with emotion and smoke. "I can't believe he turned himself in."

"Carter... I can't... what will I do?" Laura let out a long, painful moan, and for a moment, I wondered if my heart would collapse. "What will I---"

"Come here," Reid said, and he enveloped her skinny body into the warmth of his jacket. For a while, she cried into his chest, and I cried too, finally letting loose the grief and suffering that had strangled me along with everyone else that night. This had been one of the most dramatic nights of our lives. I didn't know what would happen from here. I was almost too scared to find out.

"I've got you," Reid said to Laura once she lifted her head. "No matter what happens next, I've got you."

Shocked and broken from all of it, I staggered toward both, and when I reached Reid's side, he moved so that I could hug Laura also. She was broken and bruised just as much as Reid and me.

But for the first time that night, I felt something I wasn't sure I'd ever feel again.

I felt peace.

CHAPTER TWENTY-SEVEN

Tarryn

It took firefighters from two counties almost three hours to extinguish the fire, and when they did, there wasn't much left to show for their efforts. Reid and I sat in the back of one of the Victor County fire trucks and watched them work, waiting until the last firefighter packed up to leave the scene. We didn't say much else as we watched the flames smolder.

I was in shock. Stunned. Exhausted. It had been of the longest and most impactful nights of my life. And I knew if I felt that way, Reid had to feel worse.

"Where are you sleeping tonight?" I asked when the last fire truck rolled away from the property. We stood near my car and I gestured toward it. "Let me rephrase. What I mean is, I want you to stay with me."

"At your father's house?"

"Yes." I looked at the smoldering shell of what remained of Reid's home. It was charred wood, ash, soot, and smoke. And if it looked that bad in the darkness, I couldn't imagine how scary it might appear in the morning. "He was going to sleep when I left to come here, but he needs to know what happened. He was horrified and upset at the meeting. I can only guess how upset he will be when he hears about this."

"An arson trial is pretty much the last thing anyone needs." Reid sighed and regarded the smoldering debris. "It was malicious and unjust, but also... some of Allen's most upstanding citizens came here tonight and participated in it." He rubbed the back of his neck a few times before he resumed staring off into the distance. "I don't think any of us can survive a trial like that after what we've all been through these last few years."

Reid did have a point there. It had been a long period of darkness for all the people in this region, and as a relative outsider, I couldn't understand all the dynamics.

"Fair enough," I said on a sigh. We both needed a decent night's sleep, and maybe things would seem better in the morning, once we'd recharged. "I understand that sentiment. But you're still coming home with me. We... um... we have an extra bedroom you can stay in."

He returned his attention to me. "I don't think that's a good idea, Tarryn. Your father still had some strong opinions about my family. I don't think he would appreciate waking up tomorrow to find me in his guest room."

"You have to sleep somewhere." I shivered, remembering the cold for the first time since my arrival at the property hours before. Now that the fire was out, the harsh reality of winter was making her presence known once more. "And I mean—"

"There's a motel on the highway between here and Stansview. It usually has vacancies. I'll sleep there, and then we can deal with the rest of this tomorrow."

"Okay," I replied. "And since you don't have a car, I'll drive you there myself."

"Wouldn't have expected anything less."

CHAPTER TWENTY-EIGHT

Tarryn

A short time later, I pulled Dad's car into the parking lot outside the Motel 10 on State Route 45. The property had a small check-in lobby, a twenty-four-hour diner, and a row of twenty or so rooms that had seen better days. But Reid was right. It might have been well after midnight, but the place had vacancies. Lots of them.

"Well, here you are," I said as he opened the door to Room 6. "Home sweet home. For the night, at least."

All the units had individual doors facing the parking lot. An outdated set of flowered curtains decorated a wide front window, and the room featured a spartan king-sized bed, modular desk, console, and flat-screen television. A western-themed painting hung above the bed headboard.

"Thanks for bringing me here." Reid took off his hat, coat, and gloves, then stored them in the small closet. He turned around. "It's been a long night."

"A really long one. I won't forget it." And then I frowned as the motel room light showed me just how bad the night had been for Reid's face. "Oh my God, that's going to hurt in the morning. I should have taken you to the hospital instead of here."

"It hurts, but I'm past the point of caring." He shrugged. "What's one more black eye, or bruised cheek?"

"I'm going to at least get you some ice."

Before he could protest, I snatched the plastic bucket from the table and disappeared out the door in search of the ice machine. I returned a few moments later with a full bucket and found Reid sitting on the edge of the bed, staring into space.

"Here, let's try to make this less horrible for when you wake up." I grabbed a few towels from the bathroom and wrapped one of them around some ice. When I joined Reid on the bed, I gently placed the wrapped cubes on the puffy skin beneath his eye.

"Ow," he yelped, and my heart broke. The last bit of resolve I had been using to keep myself together finally crumbled into dust.

"This is awful." I choked on the words. "This night, your house, Carter, the fire, the fights, the anger…"

Reid's hand found my arm. "It will be okay."

"Maybe things will look better when we wake up," I replied. "Maybe." But I wasn't sure I believed my words. After a night like this, things couldn't get worse, could they?

They can.

"What is this?" I whispered, halfway to a strangled sob. "Is this hell?"

"No, it's not. I've lived there for years. This... this is something better."

"How can you say that?"

"Because you're here with me, Tarryn."

Neither of us spoke for a moment. We just stared at each other.

"It's almost morning and we're both exhausted, I know that." Reid's grip tightened. "But I know one thing for certain. After tonight, I just want to move on."

"I do too."

His eyes searched my face. He moved a hand behind my neck and tangled his fingers in a few wayward strands of hair that had escaped my knit cap. "Whatever the future brings, I know it has to involve you. I can't bear it if it doesn't."

"Me either," I breathed. "I thought life was going to bring me one thing when I moved here to take care of my dad. Instead, it brought me something totally different. It brought me you."

He leaned down and kissed me. Our bodies connected, and the energy between us collided. The world around us faded. For the first time, there was only the two of us. Forget Allen, my dad's stroke, the accident, the steel plant closure, and the lingering threat of a region defined by its self-medication to dull the pain.

It left us that night.

"I love you, Tarryn," he said against the seam of my mouth.

"I love you too."

He pulled away and locked his gaze with mine. "I need to tell you something."

"Anything."

"Walter told me the truth about my father, about the plant closure."

"The truth?"

"Yes." His fingers played with my hair. "Dad's business partner caused the company's bankruptcy. Without his knowledge. He was too proud to let it be known, too stubborn to admit his business mistakes, and he kept it from Logan and me. Only a few people knew."

"Oh my God," I murmured. *What a sad reality. What a horrible position to be in.*

"This whole time, I thought he was a failure, and it made me almost *hate* him. But then Walter told me Dad felt responsible. He shut the company down only after doing everything he could to save it."

"Oh, Reid, I'm so sorry."

"Don't be. He made mistakes, but he wasn't the loser I thought he was. He was... human."

"Yes, like we all are."

He placed his forehead on mine. "And there's something else--- tonight at the fire, just as they were about to light up the house, I *heard* something, Tarryn."

I thought about that moment, when we were together in the snow, helpless to stop Carter and the rest of the mob from carrying out their crime. "Heard what?"

"I heard---I heard voices. I heard my dad, and my mom." He broke my gaze and focused on a blank section of the hotel room wall. "They spoke to me, Tarryn.

They… they released me. I know I can't change the past. But the future isn't yet written. I've been stuck for so long, I forgot that."

"I love you," I said again, even firmer that time. "I love you with my whole heart."

"I love *you*, Tarryn. I always will. You helped me live again, and I want to spend every moment of the rest of my life making sure you know it. That you know how grateful I really am."

Reid lowered his mouth to mine. His tongue parted my lips, and his tongue tangled with my own. It was a deeper, more complete kiss than the ones we'd shared in his kitchen, and as we collided, I realized my body had yearned for this kind of intimacy with him for weeks, since… since I couldn't remember when. I just knew I wanted him, as if he'd always been my destiny. I *needed* Reid Powell in my life, the same way a flower needed the sun, or a fish needed water. Yet I didn't feel reliant on him; we complemented each other in a way I'd never known before.

But even so, I pulled away. "You're… hurt. I don't want to make it worse, and—"

"Shh." He hooked his hand around my jawline, and his thumb stroked my lips, now swollen from the depth of our bond. "I'll stop us if it gets too painful." He smiled. "But for now, this is perfect."

Reid's lips met mine again, and it felt as if a pent-up hunger was finally being released. His hands were every-where and mine were too, as we stripped off the first layer of clothing. His jeans and shirt went on the floor, and mine followed, our clothing a heap of surrender to what we both wanted, what we both needed, what we both could not live without.

"Jesus Christ," he said under his breath as I unhooked my bra, then tossed it too into the pile of discarded clothing. "You're beautiful, Tarryn. The most beautiful woman I've ever seen."

Reid pulled me onto the bed. Our bodies entwined, and his mouth crushed into mine. If kissing me hurt him at all, he didn't show it—or perhaps the passion between us overrode it, taking us to places we'd never been before. I wanted that for him. I wanted him to feel free to love, free to forgive himself, free to live.

"Let me worship you," he said, then he kissed down my neck. His lips trailed kisses down my body, and when he was between my thighs, he pulled my underwear off in one smooth movement. "I was lost," he said between kisses on my thighs, my hips, and the apex of my most private place. "I was alone. I was afraid. I was consumed by guilt." He raised his head, and lazily looked at me through his scars, both visible and invisible. "But now I'm alive. I'm free. I'm no longer a captive of the pain that had imprisoned me."

Reid moved his mouth back up my body, over my stomach, then brushing each of my nipples. I moaned from the pleasure then groaned as his mouth covered mine once more, and I felt the pressure of his arousal through the cotton of his boxer shorts. "And it's all because of you."

"Please," I murmured from some place deep inside me that I didn't know existed and didn't fully understand. "I don't think I can take this. I need you inside me. Now."

He moved over me again, and I felt him hesitate. Through the fog of the moment, I understood he was worried, that he wanted to be *safe,* an unspoken question remained between us, one that had once been so far from the realm of our connection.

"It's okay," I said as I moved to press his body's weight into me. "I'm on birth control and have been for years. We'll be fine."

"Are you sure?"

"Yes."

I nearly came undone from the energy that pulsed between us, the adrenaline that buzzed through my body, and the sheer heaviness of the reality that this man—*this* man, who had locked himself away from everyone and everything—had finally opened himself to me. All defenses were down. The gates had opened. I'd stormed Reid's castle, and I hadn't only won the battle. *I'd won the man.*

"I love you, Tarryn," he said in the darkness, just before he pushed into me for the first time. "I want all my days with you."

I wanted all my days with him too.

CHAPTER
TWENTY-NINE

Tarryn

The morning light streamed through the curtains and jolted me awake. I gasped for air and didn't recognize my surroundings. I sat up in bed and found Reid under the twisted comforter. He was naked and still asleep.

Then I realized I hadn't let my father know where I was going the previous night. *Shit.* I got out of bed and found my phone in my coat pocket, which by now smelled like stale charcoal and burned wood. I'd have to get rid of it. No amount of washing would ever get out the smell of Reid's burning home. *But I can't think about that right now.*

Dad hadn't called or sent any texts, so I typed out a quick one that at least let him know I was okay. Then I gingerly tiptoed over to Reid's side of the bed and shook him awake. I hated to do it, but I didn't have much choice.

Our time in the relative safety of the hotel room wouldn't last much longer.

"It's after seven thirty," I said when he opened his eyes. "I know it's early, but I can't stay."

A soft smile floated across his bruised face. It was still swollen, and the discoloration around his left eye appeared angrier, but Reid's lip wasn't as fat as the night before, and his nose didn't look broken. "I know you can't, Tarryn. You need to get back to your dad."

"I know, but... do you think we should go to your house first? See what it looks like?"

"It's gone. There's almost nothing left." He looked away for a moment, but when his gaze returned to me, his gaze was steely, harder, and more focused. "But, yes. Let's go there, if only so we can see it."

I nodded. "And then I'll go to my father's house." I paused, considering what that might look like. Dad still didn't know the full extent of my relationship with Reid. Yes, he'd seen me with Reid at the meeting, but we were far past friendship now. This wasn't just me wanting to help someone or help the community. This was—deep. *What will he say? What will he think?* "D-do you... uh... want to come with me?"

His fingers traced a line on my thigh. "Yes. I want to tell him how I feel about you. How much you've changed my life."

"That's not the only thing that's changed," I replied, and my mind returned to the fire. "I feel like the whole world is different."

"In some ways it is." He gave my hand a squeeze then winced. "But it's not all bad."

"How are you feeling right now?" I searched his face. *Is he just masking his pain?* "You don't have to act like you're okay, if you're not—"

Reid sat up in the bed and stretched his hands a few times, clenching and unclenching his fist. "It's not great, but I'll make it." He scrunched his face. "With the help of a whole bottle of Tylenol, maybe."

"You're on." I grasped his face with both hands, wanting him to understand through the unspoken words between us that I wasn't just with him now, I was with him forever. Everything might have changed in one intense, graphic, life -altering night, but I'd never felt more alive. I gave him a smooth kiss. "Let's get dressed."

We checked out of the hotel about fifteen minutes later, drove in silence to the nearest gas station where I bought the first bottle of painkillers that I saw, then pushed on to Reid's mangled property.

"Oh my god," I said as we got out of my car together, another sob catching in my throat.

What we found took my breath away.

Reid's manicured, well-kept Victorian farm house had disappeared. I knew that when we left the night before, but something about the daylight made the reality of that loss so sharp and ugly. The charred remains couldn't hide anymore, couldn't fade into the abyss of the winter blackness. The sticks, soot, ashes, and broken glass were like markers of the most awful night of our lives. *How are we ever going to get through this? Where do we go from here?*

I thought of all the things inside the house, all the memories he'd preserved, and all the ways I knew that home had loved him when no one else had. "This is sickening. This is—"

"Like a hard reset. A reboot." Reid grabbed my hand and gave it a tight squeeze. "And exactly what I expected to find."

"Everything you care about was in there, and it's all really gone now, isn't it?"

He wrapped me in his arms. "Everything that I care about *wasn't* in there, Tarryn. *You* weren't in there."

I hung onto him and cried as another wave of grief washed over me. *This is so wrong. So unfair. So awful...* The tears flowed, and sobs racked my body as I buried my face in Reid's shoulder. I wanted to shut out the world, erase all the pain we'd endured, and stay somewhere else, somewhere far away from there.

"I wanted them to understand you," I choked out between heaving gasps. "I wanted them to see you the way that I do."

"At least I tried." Reid's hands were in my hair again, and he kissed the top of my forehead. "I did what my family—my father—would have wanted."

"Do you want to rebuild? To try to fix this?"

"I don't know. I'm not—"

And then he broke off as we heard the distinctive crunch of an approaching car. We turned toward the sound. Fear pulsed through me—*who could be coming here now, not now*—but then Reid's shoulders relaxed, and recognition crossed his face.

"It's just Walter," he said as a blue sedan rounded the final turn and arrived at the driveway. He guided me toward the car, and Walter scrambled out of it, his face pale and stricken, eyes wide, mouth hanging open.

"Reid," he croaked. "This is worse than I thought."

"It is." Reid folded the old man into hug. "But in a lot of ways, it's better too."

Walter pulled away. "I don't understand."

"I did what you wanted. What my father wished I'd do. I stood up. I tried." Reid's eyes remained fixed on Walter. "Now, I can't say I didn't."

"I heard they arrested Carter Monroe."

Reid nodded.

Walter's jaw went slack. "I still can't believe it. I can't believe anything about this. They were talking about the fire at Country Market this morning, and the fight that you had with Carter—"

"Well, I won the fight." Reid looked as if he wanted to break into a grin, but he didn't. "Let the record show that."

Walter's head swung back and forth as he took in the devastation on the property and Reid's damaged face. "Seeing this now… I should have come to the meeting last night. I should have been there." He sniffed a few times, as if choking back the natural reaction that came from seeing the twists the last twenty-four hours had taken.

"It's better you didn't." Reid pulled Walter close again for one more hug then stepped back. The two men stood shoulder to shoulder as they surveyed what remained. "You didn't need to see that, not after you said how hard it was for you when Powell Steel closed."

Walter buried his face into Reid's shoulder, muffling his next words. "Are you going to be okay, son?"

Son. Something about the way Walter said that made my heart grow warmer, despite the frigid air, and the stark bleakness of what remained from the fire. Reid had mentioned Walter a few times, but I had no idea who he really was to Reid. But it all became so clear to me, as I watched him standing with Reid. *Side by side. Unlike an employee.* He loved Reid too. We weren't all alone, this wasn't just the two of us. We had at least one ally.

But can we find any more?

"I'm Tarryn," I said when they separated. I held out my hand. "Tarryn Long."

Walter shook it, raising one scraggly eyebrow at Reid. "Necklace girl, right?"

"That's her."

"Nice to meet you," I said.

Reid took the hand I'd just used to shake Walter's. "Get used to her, okay? She's going to be around from now on."

"Good." Walter smiled wide enough to turn the wrinkles on his face to deep canyons. "I like that. Keep it up, Reid. Keep it up."

After another fifteen minutes or so at the property, we left for my dad's house. During the ride, I played the conversation I expected to have with him over and over in my mind, and by the time we pulled into the driveway, a large knot had formed in my stomach.

How are we going to explain all of this to him?

We found Dad and Nora in the living room watching a morning television show. After a quick hello, a frown crossed Dad's face. He hadn't expected this, and I knew it.

Nora's eyes were wide too. I had no other choice than to jump in with my explanation.

"Did you hear what happened last night?"

Dad shook his head.

"It wasn't on the news?"

"Your dad was so tired last night that I put him to bed and then went home," Nora said. "We just turned on the TV this morning, but the newscast was already over. And honestly, I expected you'd be back at some point last night."

"I'm… I'm sorry you were home alone overnight, Dad, but it was… let's go into the kitchen, okay? We can talk there. Reid, will you give us a minute?"

"Sure," he replied. "I can leave if you want, or—"

"No. You don't have anywhere else to go."

With Nora's assistance, I helped my dad out of the recliner and helped navigate the walker to move from one room to the next.

"I… hate… I hate this darned… thing," he muttered as we crossed the threshold from the hallway into the kitchen.

"Only a few more weeks of using it." I closed the door behind us so Reid wouldn't hear our conversation. "You're doing better than the doctors expected, and that's amazing."

I turned on the coffeemaker as I decided how to tell my father what had really happened the night before, and how far the community had gone with their anger. There was no easy way to say it. Finally, I just turned to him and Nora.

"Carter Monroe is in jail. He and a few other people burned down Reid's house last night."

"Wh—what?" My father's body slumped against the walker as if it had absorbed the shock of my words.

"Dad?" I shrieked. "Are you okay?"

Nora and I rushed to steady him, then led him to the kitchen table, where we helped him take a seat.

"Let me get you some water," Nora murmured. She moved toward the sink and filled a freshly cleaned glass from the drying rack.

I studied my dad for signs that he needed more attention. *So far, I don't see any.* "I knew this would upset you, but I wanted you to know about it. Frankly, I'm surprised you didn't already hear about it."

"Was Reid at the house at the time?" Nora asked as she handed Dad the glass of water. She'd thrown a straw in as well, and Dad took a long sip from it.

"He was. Carter rounded up a group of people last night, after the meeting. They formed a mob and set fire to Reid's place. He's lucky they didn't kill him. They intended to."

"I imagine they did. Everyone was so upset," Nora replied.

I sank into the one of the kitchen table chairs. "I don't think I'll ever understand this town. I've been trying, but I don't think I ever will."

I considered adding more, spilling what Reid had told me the night before about his father, but instead I kept that to myself. That was Reid's story to tell, his information to share, not mine.

"This town… so hurt…" Dad said.

I stared at my father for a few moments, flipping the events of the previous evening over in my mind. "He's a good person. I swear he is. He meant well last night. He wanted to help."

"That was clear during that meeting. They didn't want to listen. And he got wrapped up with Carter, and all of Carter's anger. That didn't help his case much," Nora said, rubbing her chin.

I turned my eyes to her. "That fight didn't solve anything. It made the tension worse."

"I can't believe Carter is in jail. That he committed that kind of horrific crime." She pursed her lips as she nodded. "He has always been a decent man, but I guess the stress of it all finally broke him. There's only so much one person can deal with, and he's had more than his fill."

"I just wish they'd listened last night at the community center. That they would give him a chance."

"I don't know," Nora replied. "Things are so complicated."

"I know, but... try to see this another way." I was pleading with the two of them now, pleading the case of the man I loved. Maybe if I won people over one by one, they'd see what I saw in Reid. *They must.* "Do you know what? He also saved Carter's sister a few days ago, when she overdosed."

"*He's* the one who gave her the Narcan?" Nora whispered.

I nodded. "It was him."

Dad's eyes widened. "What... did Carter... say?"

I threw up a hand. "It was after the fire. After he'd taken the whole thing into his own hands. After all of that and... Carter's sorry. He's ashamed of what he did, of the fight, and of his hardheadedness. And Reid forgives him. He just wants this nightmare to go away. But how can it, if everyone still hates him? And now---with this arson case, where do we all go from here?"

The three of us stared at each other for an eternity. I hardly breathed, it felt like whatever they said next would have a mountain of impact.

Please see the good in him, please...

"I have... idea," Dad finally remarked. "Nora, will... you... will you help me?"

"Whatever you need," she replied.

I felt breathless and beyond my own limit. I didn't have any clue what my dad meant, but I was long out of solutions anyway.

CHAPTER THIRTY

Tarryn

L eave it to my father, the prosecutor, to pull every string he had in the community. He knew everyone in town, and they respected his long history of public service, so when he contacted people, they tended to respond. Besides, he didn't often call in favors.

And so just before noon, the mayor, Victor County's sheriff, Allen's chief of police, and a few other town leaders sat in our living room, waiting for Dad to explain why he'd called them to his home on a Tuesday morning. I offered them coffee and tried to keep whatever trepidation I had at bay. All the men had expectant looks on their faces.

"Last night... another hard night," Dad began. He might have lost his booming voice, but he still had command of a room, stroke be damned. "Tarryn... told me what happened."

"It's a shame," Glen replied. "As mayor, I never expected to see a night like that."

Of course you didn't.

But I resisted the urge to vocalize my frustration. Dad had coached me beforehand on how to handle this one, and that the other people in the room wouldn't respond well to anger or threats. But it was still hard.

"And now... Carter" Dad said.

"We've got a real mess on our hands here," the police chief said. "Carter's talking down at the jail, and he's named a few other people involved, but it's all so complicated."

"My daugh... my daughter has formed... a friendship with Reid Powell," Dad said. "You... could call it... more."

"I thought you looked pretty cozy with him last night," Glen said.

"I love him. Simple as that," I said, not giving a flying flip what anyone in the room thought of those words. I wasn't going to hide my love for Reid, wasn't going to make excuses for my affection "And he deserves a chance—for people to see him in a different way. He's taken the brunt of a lifetime of anger."

"A lot of folks made up their minds a long time ago about him. And you know how people are about things like this. They're stubborn," Glen replied.

"Good thing we're... stubborn too." Dad turned his head toward the kitchen. "Reid... come out here."

A few people looked at each other again, as if in disbelief. Several men swore when they took in Reid's appearance. His face and body were a mix of angry welts and dark blue bruises. *They should be ashamed of what one of their own did to this man.*

"Reid Powell is…" Dad motioned to Nora, and she picked up where his voice and body failed him.

"Reid's staying here for the next few weeks as a guest," Nora explained. "In fact, Mr. Long hasn't told him this, but he's willing to allow Reid to stay here as long as he needs and will do whatever he can to assist him in his next endeavors."

Dad smiled at Reid. "That is… if you will let me."

"Of course I will, Mr. Long. I appreciate your support. And the offer."

Reid smiled back at him, and as he did, my heart swelled. *This* was how I'd envisioned things going the night before, at the community meeting. I'd so desperately wanted things to go well and wanted people to open their hearts up to see what had become so clear to me. Reid Powell wasn't a liability to this community or this region.

He was an asset. And I was so head over heels in love with him.

"I… I know we don't… like change." Dad commanded the full attention of the group once more. "But… we *have* to change. Change or… die. And I've talked… to Tarryn… about Reid's ideas. We owe it… to ourselves… to try his plan."

"Why would you want to stay, after what's happened here?" Glen asked Reid. "I thought you'd be gone as soon as you could. You have nothing left. They burned it all down last night."

"I thought about that," Reid said. "I considered that. I figured this place was done with me, and I was done with it." He stepped closer to me and took my hand. "But then I realized what I'd be leaving. I'd be leaving a place that nurtured me, and for what—for a big city, or a new life? For a chance at something that might not even work? My family loved this place once. They loved the beauty of this valley and the heartiness of the people in it. They saw value here, and I think I can help rediscover it. What's more, it's the *one* thing I want to do. It's the calling I've been waiting for."

I sucked in a deep breath, trying to read their expressions. I didn't know what they'd think, or if they would agree, but then the mayor nodded.

"Okay, son, we'll work with you," Glen said. "I think we've all been through enough in the last decade or so. Nothing wrong with trying to start clean."

And for the first time, I exhaled and let the significance of his acceptance wash over me. I'd come to Allen hoping I'd help my dad heal after his stroke. I'd hoped to spend time getting to know him better. But instead, Allen changed me. Reid had changed all of us.

For the better.

EPILOGUE

Six Months Later

Reid

I n a way, it all fit.

Once, the tract of land that made up Powell Steel bustled with activity. Hundreds of cars parked in the lot. The smoke stacks puffed. Shifts of uniformed workers marched through the gates for day, swing, and night shifts. Factory lights stayed on and minor traffic jams clogged the streets as the people of Victor County put their sweat behind the company.

He remembered how it had defined his childhood, how it had come together to form the beating heart of a community determined to live the American dream through a hard day's work.

Once, Powell Steel had made the region proud. But the real satisfaction hadn't come in the products the business made. It had come from the way his family and neighbors worked together to produce something greater than themselves.

And that's going to happen again.

Reid lifted the golden shovel. He'd found it a few weeks before, in the wreckage of what remained from the fire on his property. It was in the back of the burned-out storage shed, covered in soot, and one of the few things that didn't disintegrate that night. His grandfather last used it to break ground on a company expansion in the late 1970s. It hadn't been used since.

Until today.

Holding the long handle, Reid looked out at the crowd. About two hundred people peered back at him. Not as many as he'd hoped, but not a small group, either. A few television outlets from Cleveland, Pittsburgh, and Youngstown aimed their cameras at him, waiting. A photographer from the local newspaper snapped photos.

It was a start, and that mattered. It was all he'd wanted. A chance.

Reid glanced to his left. Tarryn stood about ten feet away from him, next to her father, Walter, Nora, and Laura, home on a visit from the rehab center Reid helped her get into in Pittsburgh. Tarryn wore a red lace dress and black heels. The wind blew her hair, but the sun made it shine like spun silk. It was summer now, and she looked like an angel. *My angel. The woman who saved me.* When their eyes met, she smiled.

"Thank you for coming," he told the crowd. "It's my pleasure to kick this off today, on the site of what used to be our region's largest employer."

Reid turned to the rotting factory building behind him, which had an array of broken windows, crumbling brick, and rusting metal. From where he stood, he had a straight view through the old central building to the employee parking lot. Powell Steel was a skeleton.

But soon, there would be some muscle on her bones.

"Today is the first day of the next generation of this site." His voice grew louder and stronger as he refocused on the people waiting to be a part of this moment. Many of them had accepted jobs with his company, and others had stepped in to clean up the wreckage from the fire. He studied their faces, and decided he saw something in their expressions he hadn't seen in a long time.

Hope.

"I'm proud to break ground on this new endeavor. It's my mission to make sure Powell Advanced Robotics is the premier employer in this region." He raised the shovel and pushed it into the soft earth in front of his boots. Applause rippled through the gathering, and he grinned. "This is the start of something bigger than us. And I hope you're as pleased as I am to be part of it. The past doesn't have to define us anymore. Neither does the present. Instead, we are only as small as the limits of our dreams. Our future can be better than the past. It *will* be."

He left the spade in the ground and moved closer to the people who would make up the first handful of workers at the new company. They gathered around him, forming a circle of energy.

"To a new Allen, Ohio." His words were almost a shout. "To a new Victor County."

"To a new Victor County," the crowd answered in unison.

Reid scanned the group for Tarryn. He moved closer and grabbed her hand. It was soft, warm, and reassuring.

"You did it," she said in his ear. "You're *doing* it."

"Because of you." He squeezed her palm, thinking of Logan and his parents. They might not have lived to see this day, but for once, the grief of their absence didn't wrap around his heart. Instead, he carried their memory alongside him, and used it as a spark for something better. Something brighter. "This is all because of you, Tarryn. You changed my life. And now, we're going to change the future."

"Right after I graduate from Ohio State," she replied. "So, give me a few months."

"Of course," he said as he pulled her close. "I've waited this long, so what's another few months?"

Reid drew Tarryn toward him and pressed his lips to hers. It was the kind of kiss that felt like a signature, like the final note of a long opera. He'd spent years in the barren wilderness, wondering if he'd ever see daylight again. More than once, he'd given up, and given in to the pain of his past. But now, the dawn had come. It was going to be a beautiful day.

Light had entered his life, and the future held a promise of better things.

AUTHOR'S NOTE

This book is culmination of over five years of ideas, brainstorming, and planning. For a long time, I was afraid to tell this story, and it only came about because of the tremendous support I've had from some wonderful and impactful people.

First, I'd like to thank my husband, Sean Celi, who has always offered me the unwavering encouragement I've needed to peruse this passion.

I'd also like to thank the following people, all of whom offered ideas, feedback, editorial support, and motivation for this book: Lisa Hubbard, Tasia Bade, Ainslee Gordon, Lauren McKellar, Marion Archer, Kevin Newman, Terra Newman, Karen Lawson, Christine Wheary, Jennifer Perusek, Judi Perkins, and Julie Titus.

Special thanks as well to Peter Barrett, Michelle Caruso Barrett, David Livermore, and George Zamary.

Finally, I'd like to thank these Ohio communities, all of which served as direct and indirect inspiration for this story: Youngstown, Canfield, Lordstown, Warren, Wilmington, McArthur, Adams County, and Pike County. This one is for the Buckeyes.

OTHER BOOKS BY SARA CELI